THE
$100 MILLION
TIGRESS

A WILDLIFE TALE FOR
THE CORPORATE JUNGLES!

THE $100 MILLION TIGRESS

A WILDLIFE TALE FOR THE CORPORATE JUNGLES!

SAM HANDA

ZORBA BOOKS

ZORBA BOOKS

Published by Zorba Books, July 2024
Website: www.zorbabooks.com
Email: info@zorbabooks.com

Title: **The $100 Million Tigress**
Author Name: Sam Handa
Copyright © Sam Handa
Softcover ISBN :- 978-93-5896-510-0
Ebook ISBN :- 978-93-5896-351-9

Zorba Books Pvt. Ltd. (opc)
Sushant Arcade,
Next to Courtyard Marriot,
Sushant Lok 1, Gurgaon – 122009, India

CONTENTS

CHAPTER 1

"Listen closely, my dear," Arjun began, his voice tinged with nostalgia and excitement. "The jungle, it's not just a place; it's a living, breathing entity. It's where I found my courage, faced my fears, and learned lessons no book could ever teach."

His wife, intrigued, leaned in. "But why must we go? What does the jungle hold for us?"

Arjun took her hands in his, eyes alight with the fire of conviction. "Imagine a world untouched by the chaos of our lives, where every leaf and every creature have a story to tell. I've been there before, and it changed me. It's time for us to embark on this adventure together, to discover the untamed beauty and the wisdom it holds."

She saw the earnestness in his gaze, the unwavering belief in his words. And in that moment, she knew the jungle was calling not just to him but to both of them. The flickering neon sign of Krishna Expeditions cast a weak glow in the early morning haze as Arjun and Lakshmi navigated the mist towards it.

"Why choose this place, Arjun?" Lakshmi inquired. "It seems utterly dilapidated, and I doubt their vehicles are any better. Why not opt for A2Z Explorers nearby? Their signage is far more appealing, and they are likely to have superior heating."

A subtle grin appeared on Arjun's face. "Perhaps it's the name," he replied. "A name can reveal much about a location based on the proprietor's choice. Moreover, securing a jeep here will be swift. We'll embark on our journey in no time!"

Lakshmi let out a resigned sigh. "Your fixation with Krishna never ends," she remarked. "If it weren't for your fascination with tigers, Krishna would consume all your thoughts."

"Absolutely!" Arjun proclaimed. "They are the twin foundations of my existence. One cannot exist without the other."

"Just wait until you inform the next available guide that you intend to visit Jim Corbett in such dreadful weather," Lakshmi challenged. "I wager a lakh that he'll refuse."

"We shall see," Arjun declared as he pushed open the door to the shop and entered its moist confines.

"Hello, hello, hello!" said the portly, balding man behind the counter. "Welcome to Krishna Expeditions, where all your greatest adventures begin! My name is Pranav. How can I help you today?"

"We'd like a jeep and driver," said Arjun. "We're headed to Jim Corbett National Park."

"My, my," said Pranav. "Sir, might I suggest somewhere less... exotic? It's peak tourist season right now, and the weather's been quite unpredictable lately. No telling what strangeness might come your way."

"No, we're definitely headed for the park," said Arjun. "We have quite the odyssey ahead of us, and we're more than prepared."

"I see," said Pranav. "Well, if you're absolutely certain... Manoj! Come out here, you've got passengers!"

The shop's musty silence remained undisturbed as Arjun and Lakshmi waited for the man, they assumed would take them to their destination. As seconds turned into minutes, Pranav exclaimed, "Manoj! Come, man! We haven't got all bloody day!"

A silhouette emerged from the doorless entryway to a back room, morphing into a yawning, dhoti clad man scratching his belly as he shuffled into the light. "What is it, Pranav?" he said. "Passengers, you say?"

"Yes, passengers," said Pranav. "They're headed to Jim Corbett National Park. How soon can you leave?"

"Eh?" said Manoj. "Jim Corbett? It's March and the weather's been crazy. I'm not going."

"You- what?!" Pranav spluttered, scurrying towards the man and saying in a conspiratorial whisper, "You bloody fool. How many passengers have we had this past week? That's right, two. This will make it three, and if we don't get at least three passengers in a damn week, Manoj, I'm going back to Dehradun and leaving you and the rest of you lazy jeep boys behind."

Manoj heaved a sigh. "Fine, fine," he said, turning to Arjun. "Can I at least have my breakfast before we head out?"

Arjun flashed a smile, dazzling in the gloom. "Certainly!" he said, "Take all the time you need."

***

The sun had risen considerably by the time Manoj was ready, but Arjun and Lakshmi were unconcerned by the delay. Route planning, scheduling and the general excitement of adventure were enough to help them pass the time.

"Right then," said Manoj, approaching the dusty jeep with all the enthusiasm of a man walking to the gallows. "Let's be on our way."

The driver turned the key in the ignition, the jeep spluttered to life, and the trio set off.

"It's a five-hour journey to the park," said Manoj as he exited the parking lot. "We might as well talk about something to pass the time. And I have something specific I need to ask you."

"Which is?" asked Arjun, distractedly, his eyes transfixed on the greenery around him.

"You look like such a well-to-do couple," said Manoj. "From Mumbai, I take it?"

Arjun and Lakshmi exchanged a glance and laughed. "Yes," said Lakshmi. "Is that your question?"

"Not quite," said Manoj. "My question is... wouldn't you want to go where you can put your feet up? Some fancy place where fancy folk like you tend to go?"

"Oh," said Lakshmi, "I'd better let Arjun take this one."

"It's not that complicated really," said Arjun with a chuckle. "We want to see a tiger."

"In person?" asked Manoj. "Face to face?" "Yes, indeed!" said Arjun. "One tiger in particular, actually, but I'll be happy to see any at all."

"Have you ever seen a tiger before?" asked Manoj, raising an eyebrow. "They're not like the ones you'd see at the circus. They're wild animals, so it's best to steer clear of them."

"Oh, I've seen a tiger before," said Arjun. "Long ago. Fifteen years ago, in fact. That's why I'm going back. To see if I can find her again."

"Here we go," said Lakshmi, smiling despite herself. "Strap yourself in, Manoj. He loves telling this story, no matter how many times he's told it before."

Arjun closed his eyes and began to tell the tale.

"I believe I was around 21 years old at the time," he said, "or was it 20? Besides the point. What matters is that I was young. Not so young that I was completely inept, but young enough that I hardly knew anything about the real world. I'd just graduated from college, and everyone told me the world was my oyster, but I just didn't understand what I was expected to do."

"An understandable situation," said Manoj.

"I found my escape in films," Arjun continued, "often staying back to watch the same picture twice and sometimes three times in one night. They gave me comfort, but they were also a major distraction. Of course, I didn't care at the time. I just didn't want to think about that big, scary future everyone wanted me to focus on."

"Sounds nothing like the man I know today!" giggled Lakshmi.

"One day, I saw this film. What was its name? I'm shocked I can't remember, honestly, because the film itself was spectacular. It was about a tiger that kept attacking a village and a brave warrior that set out to kill it. I thought the movie would be fairly predictable. The hero tracks the beast, battles it for some time, and eventually slays it. Big finish, everybody claps."

Arjun leaned forward and locked eyes with Manoj through the rearview mirror. "But that's not what happened at ALL."

"So what happened, then?" Manoj asked.

"Instead," said Arjun, "the hero finds the tiger. It turns out to be a tigress and behind her, he sees the cubs. He realizes, and this is very important so listen carefully, he realizes that she's not trying to attack the village. She's trying to feed her babies."

Arjun's eyes widened and glazed over. He was far away now, tumbling back through time.

"You see, the villagers would go hunting quite often, and they'd get a bit overzealous, if you know what I mean. Killing one deer is reasonable, but kill four at a time and you're depriving a predator of its prey. Of *course* she ventured into the village. She was just looking for food!"

"And is that why you want to see the tiger?" asked Manoj. "After all these years?"

"No," said Arjun. "Like I said. I've seen one before, and it was all because of this film. The tigress on the screen was so magnificent, I just had to see one with my own two eyes, so I scrounged up every penny I could find and booked myself a trip to Jim Corbett National Park."

"And that's where it happened," said Lakshmi, looking at her husband adoringly.

"That's where it happened," said Arjun, meeting Lakshmi's gaze with a smile. "It took a while, of course," he said, turning back to Manoj. "It took days. I cut my arm on a branch, I nearly broke my ankle, it was a real adventure, you know? There were snakes. But at the end of it, I came upon a clearing, and in this clearing was the most unimaginably beautiful tiger. I kept my distance, but I got close enough to get a good look at her. It's one thing to see it in a movie, but to see it in real life? Magical. And do you want to know what the most amazing thing is?"

"What?" asked Manoj, his eyes flitting from road to rearview.

"She was surrounded by her little cubs," said Arjun, slapping his knee and letting out a hearty guffaw. "It was like I was in that movie! I couldn't believe my eyes. These little, perfect creatures, tumbling over each other, play fighting and chasing their own tails. It was the most perfect thing I'd ever seen."

"I see," said Manoj. He opened his mouth as if to say something, then shut it as though he'd reconsidered. "Well, we'll be there in around four and a half hours. Then you'll have plenty of time to look for this tigress of yours."

"Oh, I intend to," said Arjun, curling his fingers into Lakshmi's and gazing at the passing scenery. "No matter what."

CHAPTER 2

Mr. Krishna burst into the conference room, his brow furrowed in a way all too familiar to the employees of Maverick Software Solutions.

"Right, team", he said, adjusting his glasses and addressing the dozen or so young executives seated around the table, into the speakerphone in the center. "Can everyone hear me okay? Sebastian? Daniel?"

The head of the Philippines sales team and his American

software architect responded, saying they could hear him loud and clear. Mr. Krishna turned to Salman, his business advisor, and gave him a conspiratorial wink before continuing.

"So it's looking like Project 100 Million Tigress is well on its way," he said.

"Definitely," said Sebastian, his faint Texas twang taking on a sardonic tone as he continued, "although I still don't quite understand the name."

"Names are important," said Mr. Krishna with a laugh. "We're all tigers and tigresses here. We have to be if we're going to hit our revenue goals for the year, Mighty $100 Mn."

Mr. Krishna's gaze swept across the room, each team member feeling the weight of his vision. "This year, we're not just aiming high, we're doubling down," he declared with a steely resolve. "We're setting our sights on a 100% growth. It's a bold move, one that will require every ounce of our combined efforts, innovation, and dedication."

Salman shifted uncomfortably in his seat, saying, "45% growth in a single year is a tall order. Though we have made considerable progress in a short time. But is it possible to sustain it?"

"We are on the right track," said Mr. Krishna, contemplatively stroking his salt and pepper beard, his furrowed brow deepening as he locked eyes with Salman'. His bright tone of voice revealed nothing of the storm clouds gathering behind his eyes.

Mr. Krishna concluded with a rallying cry that echoed off the conference room walls, "We're not just growing; we're transforming. By this time next year, Maverick Software Solutions will have doubled its market presence, its revenue, and most importantly, its impact. Let's make this leap together!"

As Mr. Krishna surveyed the room, his voice took on a determined edge. "Our strategy is clear," he began. "We're not just scaling; we're revolutionizing our approach. We've mapped out a meticulous plan that hinges on aggressive market penetration and leveraging cutting-edge technology to double our growth within the next fiscal year."

Salman nodded in agreement, his analytical mind already running through the logistics. "It's a bold vision, but with our strategic partnerships and innovative marketing campaigns, we're poised to not only meet but exceed our ambitious target,' he added confidently."

Mr. Krishna's eyes gleamed with the reflection of a well-laid plan. "We've identified key growth drivers and allocated resources accordingly. Our roadmap includes expanding our service offerings and streamlining operations to ensure that our trajectory towards 100% growth is not only achievable but sustainable."

Mr. Krishna, with a confident nod to his team, outlined the next phase of the growth strategy. "First up, we're taking our Food App global, starting with a major launch in the Philippines. It's a vibrant market, hungry for innovation, and we're ready to serve up success."

Finally, Mr. Krishna unveiled the game-changer. "Time is of the essence, and we're setting a new standard with our 15-minute delivery service for restaurant food. Fast, reliable, and on the dot—that's our promise."

"It's all about keeping an eye on the markets," he continued, his eyes clearing up. "Ride sharing is the name of the game these days. It's a pathway into all sorts of new revenue streams. Especially when we expand aggressively. We all knew that the Philippines was ripe for the taking! And thanks to Daniel, we now have a foothold there. How's the home food delivery feature rollout going, Radha?"

"I'd say so-so," said the product manager. "We're at 67%

adoption already, and it's only been a month. Not a ton of revenue as yet, but it'll help keep the momentum going."

"Any issues with app functionality?" asked Mr. Krishna. "Well, to be honest, there have been some complaints of app crashes," said Radha.

"Not ideal," said Mr. Krishna, stroking his beard again, "but not unexpected. Sebastian, could you take a look at things under the hood? Crashes shouldn't be happening."

"Yes sir, Mr. Krishna," said Sebastian, "I'll have the team look into it right away."

"Please do," said Mr. Krishna, "we don't have any time to lose. Mukesh, how is the restaurant outreach?"

"I've sent out feelers to local chains like you asked," said Mukesh. "It's helping to get the big fish onboard, your KFCs and McDonald's, and what have you. You were right on that front. Now that we've widened our net, I feel we'll have at least twenty more restaurants on the platform by the end of the week."

"Hmm," said Mr. Krishna, finally settling down into his chair and pondering his steepled fingers. "I'll have a think about where we can go from there. Good work, though, Mukesh. Everyone, in fact. Daniel, anything to report from Manila?"

"Rollout is going as expected, sir," said Daniel. "We've added a hundred thousand more users this past week, so revenue should keep climbing. That said, we might be plateauing soon. It's hard to tell when that might happen."

"We'll cross that bridge when we get to it," said Mr. Krishna. "Sounds like everything's going according to plan, more or less. Thank you, everyone, for indulging me during these meetings. I know you're all busy, and it might seem to you that we can cover this in an email, but meeting face-to-face helps get everyone on the same page quickly. In the case of Sebastian and Daniel, it's good to hear their voices in real-time. Alright, that's it for today, everyone. Have a nice day."

The team began to disperse through the glass doors and meandered back to their desks. Mr Krishna placed a hand on Salman's shoulder as he got up.

"Stay back a minute," he said. "I need to talk to you."

Salman straightened his back and clasped his hands on the desk, his posture as crisp as his spotlessly white dress shirt. There was a tenseness there, a nervous anticipation of what his boss might say, but Salman knew it'd be something he needed to hear.

"Listen, Sal," said Mr. Krishna. "I understand that you have some reservations about our goal, you've brought them up countless times, but could you avoid bringing them up at team meetings?"

The tone of his voice was soft but firm, yet Salman winced. As much as he tried to steel himself for a rebuke, it always stung to know that the man he admired was disappointed in him.

"I'm not angry with you, Sal," said Mr. Krishna, placing his hand back on his business advisor's shoulder. "It's just that comments like that don't go unnoticed. We're doing well now, but if we're ever in a slump, team members will recall what you said and start to lose hope."

"I didn't mean to sap anyone's morale," said Salman. "I should've focused on the matter at hand instead of fretting. I know that sir, it's just that..."

"You're worried we can't do it," said Mr. Krishna as Salman trailed off. "It's an understandable concern, which is why I don't fault you for having it."

"Sir," said Salman, "if I may speak freely. Revenue is trending up because we aggressively expanded into a new market, and you were spot on about the demand in Manila, but..."

"Go on," said Mr. Krishna, leaning back into his chair and staring intently at his business advisor.

Salman cleared his throat. "There are two ways I see this ending," he said-

Mr. Krishna had turned his head, but only so his ear was aimed directly at Salman. Realizing he should keep talking, Salman continued, "On one end of the spectrum, our growth rate may hold steady. It could even increase, but managing that growth will be a nightmare in itself. The logistical problems alone will require significant resources, both in terms of money and manpower."

"And since you're my business advisor, I'm assuming you've thought of a solution before bringing this up?" said Mr. Krishna, his eyes twinkling, the corners of his mouth curling.

"Yes, sir," said Salman. "We need to bring in a consultant. Someone outside the company, someone that can take a bird's eye view and tell us where and when we should place our bets."

"Interesting," said Mr. Krishna.

"I know I'm your business advisor," said Salman. "I know I'm supposed to be the one to take you to the finish line, and I'm sorry if I'm failing at that."

"It's not a failure to know when you need help," said Mr Krishna. "You're absolutely right. We poached Sebastian and his team specifically because they had experience in a larger company in the field. We needed their experience in expanding the app's reach, so it was just a matter of time before we needed someone else on the business side of things."

"So you agree?" said Salman, the tension from his shoulders dissipating at last.

"Definitely," said Mr. Krishna. "To catch a tiger, you need help from someone who knows the jungle better than you do. Will you reach out to someone, then?"

"I have a few candidates in mind," said Salman. "I'll get in touch with them and bring someone on board in a few days. And, sir, just because I'm nervous doesn't mean I don't have faith in you. I know we'll get there. I know we'll win."

"Oh, I intend to," said Mr. Krishna, slowly rising from the chair. "No matter what."

CHAPTER 3

They were two hours into the journey to Jim Corbett National Park. Arjun brushed his windswept hair off his face and turned to Lakshmi, saying, "Thank God you packed the binoculars."

"I knew you'd forget," said Lakshmi, smirking. "You were too focused on the camera."

"There's a metaphor in there somewhere," said Arjun, rubbing his stubble. "Also, I really need to shave."

"You'll get plenty of time when we get there," said Lakshmi. "What was that about a metaphor?"

"Oh, I don't know," said Arjun. "Something about me wanting to capture the tiger in all its glory so badly that I forgot I need to spot it first. Its prey will call out from a distance, so the best we can hope for is to get a look at it from far away and slowly walk in its general direction."

"Tiger spotting is going to take ages," Lakshmi moaned.

"I know," said Arjun, his eyes twinkling. "It'll be great."

"Not to mention exhausting," said Lakshmi, grabbing the jeep door as a bump in the road nearly sent her skyward.

"She has a point," said Manoj, breaking out of his long-drive reverie for one of his intermittent interjections.

"Well, we should probably come up with a schedule," said Arjun.

"Did you not think of this before?" Manoj grumbled. "Tiger sightings are no joke, they require a lot of planning."

Arjun grinned at that, locking eyes with Manoj in the rearview. "It was a spur of the moment decision. I just felt the call of the jungle and had to respond."

"No better time to plan than the present," said Lakshmi. "How about we figure out a schedule right now? We have at least a good three hours left to go."

"Sure," said Arjun, once again scratching at his stubble. "The guesthouse will be home base, obviously. We'll need a day to recover, but we can begin our search the next morning. Perhaps the best course of action is to venture out after breakfast and try a different route each day. That way, we can cover as much of the forest as possible."

"How would we know where to start, though?" asked Lakshmi.

"We listen to the sounds of the jungle," said Arjun. "More specifically, we keep an ear out for monkeys. Most prey are helpless when they see a tiger. The predator is just too close, and the best they can manage is one final distress call before it pounces, which I doubt we'll be able to hear.

Monkeys are different. They're up in the trees, so they have a chance to get away and alert the rest of their group that a tiger is approaching."

"That makes sense," said Lakshmi. "So when we hear a monkey call, we head towards it. Right?"

"Right!" said Arjun, sliding his arm around his wife's shoulders and pulling her close. "It'll take some trial and error, but eventually, we'll narrow down the terrain until the tiger's turf is all that remains."

"But what if we don't hear anything?" asked Lakshmi.

"There are more signs to look out for," said Arjun. "Tigers

mark their territory by slashing at tree trunks, so we could check any trees we pass. As soon as we see claw marks, I'd bet a tiger will be nearby."

"That sounds so dangerous, Arjun," said Lakshmi, her eyes widening. "I don't think I realized just how risky this is until now."

"Not to worry, darling," said Arjun, tightening his embrace. "I'll keep you safe. Besides, taking risks is the key to achieving success in life. The bigger the risk, the bigger the reward."

Lakshmi put her hand on Arjun's face, gave it an amicable shove and said, "You sound like a self-help book."

Arjun's laughter sounded like a bell, echoing in the grassy fields on either side.

***

"Well, would you look at that," said Arjun. "We're here!"

"What?" said Lakshmi, rubbing her eyes as she woke up from her nap and checked her watch. "Already? But it hasn't even been four hours, I thought it would take five!" She sat up and surveyed the massive tree line fast overtaking the horizon, vibrant green as far as the eye could see.

"Manoj deserves all the credit," said Arjun, slapping the driver on the back. He responded with a weary smile, met Arjun's gaze with tired eyes and said, "I just wanted to get the job done as fast as possible."

"Done?" asked Arjun, laughing incredulously. "Why, whatever do you mean, old boy?" Manoj looked at him, eyebrow raised. "I don't understand the question."

"What makes you think the job is done?" asked Arjun, leaning forward intently. "Aren't you going to take us into the forest?"

"What?!" Manoj spluttered. "Of course not!"

It was now Arjun's turn to raise a quizzical brow. "Why would we rent a jeep if we just wanted to get to the edge of the park? The whole point was that you'd take us into the heart of the area and be with us the whole time. I thought that's what we're paying you for!"

"No, no," said Manoj, shaking his head furiously. "Absolutely not. There will be rain soon, way more than usual for this time of year. No telling what might happen. It's too big of a risk."

"Manoj," said Arjun, wedging himself between the front seats and turning to face the driver. "I know you zone out sometimes, so you might not have heard what I said about risk, but it's what makes life worth living. Don't you want to see this tiger with us? You've been our trusted companion for just a few hours, but I feel like we were destined to accomplish this together."

Manoj squinted at the road and resumed his stoic silence. "If it's a question of money," said Arjun, "we will, of course, compensate you for all of the extra time."

"It's not that," said Manoj. "I just don't want to be in all that rain, trudge through all that mud. I'd rather head back home and come pick you up in a couple of weeks when you're done."

Arjun's face darkened, and Lakshmi's eyes widened as they flitted between her husband and the driver.

"You can't do this to us!" said Arjun, his voice rising to a shout. "We would've never hired you if we knew you were going to just bail on us at the last minute!"

"Arjun," said Lakshmi. "It's fine, we'll figure it out." "No we bloody won't," said Arjun. "The man's just being difficult."

"Oh go to hell," said Manoj. "You know this is too dangerous for me, you're trying to put me at risk all because you saw some film with a tiger in it decades ago."

Arjun nearly stood up in the moving jeep, but as he opened his mouth to let out a flurry of insults, Lakshmi leaned forward and pressed her mouth to his ear. The feel of her lips calmed him down somewhat, and he heard her whisper, "Arjun, darling, you know this isn't the way. Why rile him up?"

Arjun sat back down and looked at her. She told him everything he needed to hear through her eyes and without a single word. He breathed deeply, filling his lungs with so much air that it was almost uncomfortable, and said, "Tell me something, how much of your life have you spent at home?"

"What kind of a question is that?" Manoj sputtered, "I have half a mind to drop you off here and let you walk the rest of the way."

Arjun looked at Lakshmi, almost begging her to let him bulldoze the stubborn driver, but she looked back with her mouth set and her jaw clenched and he understood. Anger was not the way.

"Look, Manoj," said Arjun. "I'm sorry I lost my cool. You're right. Heading into the forest is a big risk for you."

"You're damn right it is," said Manoj, gripping the steering wheel so hard his knuckles turned white. "And I'm not doing it, so don't bother trying to convince me."

"I'm not trying to do anything," said Arjun. "I just asked you a question. Just hear me for a second. How much of your life have you spent at home?"

After a few seconds of strained silence, Manoj shrugged and said, "Most of it, I guess. Just like everyone else."

"And you have no problems with being like everyone else?" Arjun asked, his voice taking on a deeper, more serious tone.

"Of course not," said Manoj." "And what do you do when you get bored?" asked Arjun. Manoj shrugged. "Watch a movie, I guess."

Arjun's eyes widened. "Have you never wanted to see what's out there? What sorts of new and amazing adventures you could have? I saw a tiger in a film, Manoj, and then I saw it in real life. Let me tell you, the life you live from behind a screen is nothing, I repeat, NOTHING compared to the life you can have in the real world. We're going to see a tiger, Manoj, a real-life tiger prowling in its natural environment. Trust me when I say it WILL be glorious. It will change your life!"

"I don't know," said Manoj. "It just seems like such a big risk." "Do you have children?" asked Arjun.

"I don't know how that's any of your business," said Manoj, his fury cooling into embers of annoyance. "But yes, I have three."

"And when they grow up," Arjun continued, "do you want them to remember you as a man who just sat in front of a TV all day? Or do you want them to know their father was a man who saw things that defy description, things for which there are simply no words?"

Manoj contemplated the road.

"Every father wants their kids to see him as a hero," said Arjun. "I'm asking you to be *my* hero, Manoj."

Several tense seconds passed. Arjun peered at Lakshmi, uncertain. All of a sudden, the silence was broken by a rumbling, unhindered, heaving laugh emerging from somewhere in Manoj's diaphragm and spilling out of an open, joyous mouth.

"Bloody hell," said Manoj. "Are you a salesman or what?"

"Does that mean I've sold you on the idea?" asked Arjun, grinning.

"Perhaps you have," said Manoj. "I'll stick around for a few days and see how it goes."

"Brilliant," said Arjun, his night black eyes peppered with the twinkle of a thousand stars, each one a dream, a memory, a belief, each one buoyed by his insatiable desire to take the inexhaustible variety of life and swallow it whole.

The jeep screeched to a halt. Arjun looked up at the tree line, massive, mythical, mighty. He turned back to Lakshmi, awestruck, and said, "Bloody brilliant."

CHAPTER 4

Mr. Krishna leaned forward, his hands clasped together as if to unveil a secret strategy. "We're at a pivotal point, and it's time we brought in some fresh eyes," he announced. "That's why we're bringing a consultant on board—a seasoned strategist who'll help us navigate the complexities of our ambitious growth plan."

Salman, always the pragmatist, nodded in approval. "A consultant could offer us the perspective we need to fine-tune our approach and ensure we're not just growing, but growing smartly," he mused.

Mr. Krishna smiled, "Exactly, Salman. This consultant isn't just any advisor; he is the compass to guide us through uncharted territories. With his expertise, we'll not only reach our goal of doubling our size but do so with precision and foresight."

"Mr. Chetan will be arriving just after lunch," said Salman, unwrapping the cloth covered lunchbox he brought from home every day.

"Very well," said Mr. Krishna, crossing his legs and leaning back as he dipped into his goat cheese and chickpea salad, placing his other elbow casually on the arm rest. "We'll lay out the plan for him and see what he has to say."

"Hello, everyone!" said Radha as she entered the break room, her cheerful greeting accompanied by the alluring aroma of her samosa chaat.

"Treating ourselves today, are we?" asked Krishna, smiling as he glanced at her meal and gesturing towards the vacant chair around the table he and Salman were sharing.

Radha, delighted at the chance to lunch with her boss, settled down into the chair, saying "Oh, I know I probably shouldn't, but I just can't help myself sometimes. Not everyone can be as disciplined as you, sir!"

Mr. Krishna waved a dismissive hand. "At my age, you have to start eating sensibly. No choice, really. I ate far worse than samosa chaat at your age, Radha, trust me."

Radha beamed and placed a forkful of the savory mixture into her mouth, chewing it with relish. She noticed Mr. Krishna looking at the food intently.

"Would you like a bite, sir?" asked Radha, sheepishly offering a spare fork.

"Hmm?" said Mr. Krishna distractedly, "Oh, no. I was actually wondering where you got this from."

"Just from downstairs," said Radha. "There's a stall a few minutes up the road. He's my regular chaat guy. I go to him every one or two weeks."

"That's quite a hike with all the traffic," said Mr. Krishna, depositing his fork into the salad, placing his elbow on the table and resting his chin atop his fist. "Interesting. Is the chaat worth the walk?"

"Well, it's not the best chaat I've ever had," said Radha, "but it's a nice change of pace, and I don't mind the walk."

"Interesting," said Mr. Krishna, unclenching his fist and unfurling his fingers for a customary beard stroke.

"It looks delicious, Radha," said Salman, eyeing his boss and laughing uncertainly. "I should probably go try it sometime."

"Good luck getting there," said Mr. Krishna, gripping his face between his index finger and thumb. "Between the traffic and the non-existent sidewalk, it's a miracle that fellow gets any customers at all."

Radha and Salman exchanged a confused look, laughed nervously again and began to eat their meals, while Mr. Krishna did little but stare at his own.

****

Salman and Radha headed to the conference room, chatting happily while Mr. Krishna followed them slowly, hands in his pockets, eyes fixed firmly on the ground as he walked. His contemplative stroll was interrupted by the smell of cologne so strong it made his eyes water, and the sudden appearance of a man in his path dressed in a sky-blue Oxford shirt buttoned all the way to the top despite the lack of a tie.

"Mr. Krishna I presume," said the man, extending his hand. Mr. Krishna grasped it slowly, eyeing the man up and down, saying, "And you are?"

"I'm Chetan!" said the man, beaming. "Thought I'd take you aside before we headed into the conference room so we can get to know each other in a slightly less public arena."

"Oh, of course," said Mr. Krishna, still not quite back from his reverie but grasping the man's hand more tightly nonetheless. "You're the consultant."

"That I am!" said Chetan, smoothing out his shirt once Mr. Krishna relinquished his hand. "Quite the grip you've got there."

Mr. Krishna smiled. "The stars have aligned, it seems. I just had an idea that needs a consultant's input."

"Great!" said Chetan. "Fire away, I'm all ears."

"Actually," said Mr. Krishna, extracting his other hand from his pocket and gesturing towards the glass conference room door, "I was hoping I could bring it up in front of everyone. I'd like to know what they all think too."

"Oh," said Chetan, his face falling slightly. "Well, I suppose that makes sense. We can have our one-on-one chat later."

"Sure," said Mr. Krishna distractedly, already heading to the conference room. He walked in through the door with Chetan scurrying behind him and placed his hands on the backrest of one of the chairs.

"Everyone," said Mr. Krishna, "this is Chetan, our new consultant. He'll be helping us out with some of the finer details of Project 100 Million Tigress."

"Hello, all!" said Chetan, his eyes moving over the sea of occupied seats, spotted one empty seat at the far end of the table. "Pleasure to meet you, can't wait to see what we can achieve together. At the risk of sounding presumptuous, do you think you all could slide up a bit so I can sit up here next to the boss?"

Mr. Krishna squinted at the consultant, saying, "Normally it's first come, first served here, Chetan. But I guess we can make an exception this one time."

"Right, right," said Chetan with a sheepish laugh. "I would've been here earlier, except I just... well I wanted to meet you outside and... oh, well, never mind, we can clear it up later."

He settled into the newly vacated chair as the various team members rearranged themselves to accommodate him, leaned back and crossed his legs, looking at Mr. Krishna intently. If he felt at all embarrassed about the encounter, the laugh had been the only indication. He now looked calm and poised as the boss began to speak.

"So," said Mr. Krishna, "I've had an idea, and I think it's a good one, but I need you all to give me your unfiltered thoughts."

His words were met with anticipatory silence, as all eyes

remained fixed on the company leader as he slowly put his idea into words.

"I noticed today that Radha went out to get herself a treat for lunch," said Mr. Krishna, his eyes focusing and moving from executive to executive to draw them in. "It was chaat. Quite good, actually. But I realized that she had to go on quite a hike to get it. Now, the fellow selling the chaat probably does alright for himself after all, he's in the business district. There are plenty of people like Radha who'd brave the traffic to buy from him, but what about the rest of the city."

The executives looked at each other uncertainly, as Mr Krishna unveiled his new business strategy. Radha shifted uncomfortably in her seat.

"How many such street vendors are there in this city alone?" Mr. Krishna continued. "A thousand? Two thousand?"

"Umm," said Salman, leaning forward to place his hands on the conference table, "I could look into that for you if you like, sir."

"Yes, please do," said Mr. Krishna, "because I think we should work on bringing each and every one of them on our app."

A murmur rippled through the team. Chetan's eyes narrowed, a slight smile curving his lips, and kept his gaze fixed on the boss.

"Now, now," said Mr. Krishna. "Let me hear what you have to say too. Don't be afraid to speak boldly."

"Well," said Radha, "I think it's a very unique concept. Most food delivery apps either go for established chains or local restaurants. I don't think anyone has done street vendors yet."

"It would send our vendor sign-ups through the roof," said Salman. "That'd look very good on our quarterly reports."

"There's a considerable time investment involved," said

Mukesh, "but I think I can manage it while we wait for responses from the larger vendors."

"Question!" said Chetan, smiling widely and raising his hand. "Go ahead," said Mr. Krishna, crossing his arms.

"How exactly will you onboard these street vendors?" said the consultant. "I doubt many of them have electricity. They run their businesses out of stalls."

"Good point," said Mr. Krishna. "Of course, they won't really need electricity at all times. We provide each vendor with a tablet, and if they just keep that tablet charged, they can receive orders like any restaurant."

"Question!" said Chetan, continuing after Mr. Krishna gave him a terse nod, "Where will all these tablets come from?"

"We have at least five hundred tablets still available," said Radha. "Even if we keep eighty percent for bigger vendors down the line, that's still at least a hundred we could use for this experiment."

"Question!" said Chetan, raising his hand for a third time.

"You don't have to say that every time, Chetan," said Mr. Krishna, crossing his ankles and returning his hands to the chair's backrest in front of him. "Just say what you're thinking."

Chetan spread his hands and swiveled in his chair to face the team. "So, is this an experiment?"

"Indeed, it is," said Mr. Krishna.

"Well you didn't exactly specify that," said Chetan.

"We do a lot of experiments here," said Mr. Krishna. "That's how we figure out what works."

"Hmm," said Chetan, pursing his lips. The team's eyes now rested on him as he said, "Is this really the time to be rocking the boat?"

"I'd say this is the precise time to rock the boat," said Mr. Krishna. "We're aiming for rapid, exponential growth. That only happens if you try new things."

"I understand," said Chetan, raising his hands as if in surrender. "It's definitely worked well for you so far. The transition to food delivery was inspired, and it's helped you start developing a truly global footprint."

"So what exactly is the problem then?" Mr. Krishna, his voice rising to an uncharacteristically high volume.

Chetan straightened, seeming taken aback. "Why, I'm just trying to point out potential flaws in the plan," he said, gesturing towards himself as he spoke and swiveling side to side in his chair.

"Right," said Mr. Krishna. "Everybody, thank you all for coming to the meeting. Let's meet back here in three hours after some brainstorming."

"So... we're dismissed?" asked Salman, his eyes flitting between the boss and the consultant.

"For now," said Mr. Krishna, locking eyes with Chetan

who smiled back at him and crossed his arms. The executives streamed out, but Chetan remained seated and Salman lingered in the doorway.

"Are you sure you don't need anything else, sir?" asked Salman, still nervously shifting his gaze between the two men.

"Not now, Salman," said Mr. Krishna, his own gaze unwavering. "Chetan and I need to have a talk."

CHAPTER 5

Arjun gently scraped the wet blade against his foamy cheek, carefully separating the rough stubble from its roots. Finding an appropriate guest house had been no trouble at all, but convincing Manoj to actually venture out into the forest was another matter entirely, so the trio had spent the night indoors to recover from the journey and hoped to make another stab at it the following morning.

"Why shave?" asked Manoj as he watched Arjun perform his daily morning ritual.

"Why not?" joked Arjun, giving the driver a congenial glance through the mirror.

"Well, you're in the wilderness now," said Manoj. "Things are going to get messy. I'd have assumed you'd let your beard grow out."

"It's all about discipline, Manoj," said Arjun, wiping the shaving foam off his face and dipping the razor in a cup of water to rinse it off.

"That and he absolutely *hates* having a beard," said Lakshmi, gazing at her husband admiringly from the sofa.

Arjun laughed. "I just like to feel as clean as possible. Beards attract a lot of dirt, they require scrubbing to clean. Besides, shaving helps me calm myself and sort through my thoughts at the start of the day."

"There," he said, patting his cheek dry. "That's better. Now, it's 10 AM. The gate will be open. Shall we head into the forest?"

"Sure," grumbled Manoj. "Absolutely!" said Lakshmi, jumping up from the sofa.

***

Arjun sat on the stump of a felled tree and contemplated his surroundings. Never before had he seen such endless, unsurpassed beauty stretching as far as the eye could see.

"About time we took a break," said Manoj, gasping as he set down his pack and gingerly placed his behind on a suitably flat rock.

"We've been walking for all of fifteen minutes, Manoj!" laughed Lakshmi as she strolled between the trees, looking up at the foliage obscuring the sky.

"Wait," said Arjun, standing up all of a sudden.

"What?" asked Lakshmi, eyeing her surroundings warily.

Arjun shushed her by bringing a finger up to his lips. He listened intently, as did Lakshmi and Manoj, and through the thick silence of the forest permeated only by the faintest rustling of leaves, they heard, clear as the whistling of an oncoming train, the shrieking call of a monkey.

"That's it!" said Arjun. "Bloody hell, barely fifteen minutes in and we've already gotten our first sign!"

He began rushing towards the sound before turning around and seeing Manoj still squatting on the rock. "Up, Manoj, up! We haven't had a minute to waste!"

Manoj sighed pointedly, begrudgingly picked up his pack and followed Arjun and Lakshmi as they raced towards the tiger's prey. It sounded positively terrified in its warning calls, and the screams came at regular intervals as the monkey tribe warned each other of the dangers below.

After a good five minutes of sprinting, Arjun stopped in his tracks and bent over gasping. "This won't work," he said. "Of course not. The sound seems close but it must be further away than we think."

"I wish you'd thought of that before making me run with five kilos on my back!" Manoj moaned.

"Arjun," said Lakshmi, supporting her lower back with her palms and staring in the direction of the sounds. "We should check the map."

"Yes!" said Arjun. He slid his backpack off and pulled out a crisp map of the forest, placing a finger on a specific point and saying, "The guesthouse is here. We have travelled north, so we should be around here. The sound seems to be coming from the east. What's east of here?"

"More forest," said Manoj. Arjun pursed his lips, trying his best to mask his annoyance. "Question," Manoj continued, raising a finger. "Why did we leave the jeep behind?"

"Because this was just a quick outing to catch our bearings," said Arjun. "If I'd known we'd hear a call so soon, we would've obviously stayed in the jeep."

"We live and we learn," said Lakshmi.

"Monkeys have gone quiet now," said Arjun, tilting his head.

"Why don't we just circle back to the jeep and head east?" Lakshmi asked. "If there's a tiger around, I bet it's somewhere in that direction."

"Yeah," said Arjun disappointedly. "I supposed we should."

"Not like we have much of a choice," said Manoj. "Should I get back up again?"

"Yes, Manoj," said Arjun, his tone turning icy. "You will need to get up so we can explore a bit more."

"Very well," said the driver with another long-suffering sigh. "I'm just saying, this isn't exactly in my job description."

Arjun snorted and looked at Lakshmi who shook her head.

Was it a mistake bringing him along? He wondered. *Maybe I would've been better off alone.*

He looked around at the vast forest and thought, *No. Terrain is too treacherous. We need him, but maybe that's only because we brought him along. Maybe I should've been more independent...*

Lakshmi placed a hand on his arm, breaking him out of the reverie. He realized it was beside the point. They had to keep going.

"Do you know what you need?" said Manoj. "A tracker. Someone who actually knows the jungle and can read the signs."

"I can read the signs perfectly well," snapped Arjun. "We just needed you for the jeep. The tracking, I can do myself. Alright, then. On we go. We have a tiger to catch."

CHAPTER 6

Mr. Krishna stared at Chetan, tapping his fingers on the conference table as the consultant eyed him back. "I don't appreciate the way you're shooting down ideas," he said.

"I'm sorry," said Chetan, raising an eyebrow, "but didn't you hire me so that I could point out flaws in your strategy?"

"There's a difference between pointing out flaws and being a naysayer," said Mr. Krishna. "If you feel like the strategy won't work, I'd at least appreciate some details."

"Very well," said Chetan. "It's an interesting idea, bringing street vendors on board. It has its fair share of pros, including boosting your vendor sign up numbers and improving revenue projections."

Mr. Krishna pinched the bridge of his nose, squeezing his eyes tightly shut as he let out a long suffering sigh. "You have a really bad habit of beating around the bush. Get to your point. Quickly."

"The main issue I can see here is that it's uncharted territory," said Chetan. "I have to wonder, is the timing right for something like that? You've seen the market conditions. Food delivery and ride share are both on the rise, but that's only for tried and tested services. The market simply isn't ready for an experiment."

"I've been in situations where the timing wasn't right," said Mr. Krishna. "You can't just sit around and wait for the right moment, sometimes you have to take the initiative and let the chips fall where they may."

"So what you're saying is, we should just stumble ahead blindly and hope for the best," said Chetan, smirking smugly.

"That's not at all what I'm saying and you know it," said Mr. Krishna, raising an accusatory finger. "Expanding into food delivery was a risk as well. I'm sure that if you were here at the beginning you'd have dissuaded us from diverging from our so-called 'tried and tested' ride share service," he continued, making air quotation marks with his fingers for emphasis.

"I would have," said Chetan, "because my main job is to mitigate risk."

"And my main job is to take risks," said Mr. Krishna. "There's a fundamental misunderstanding here. You don't get to tell me what I can or can't do. You're here to understand my strategy and help me reach my goals."

"With all due respect, I'm not going to sit idly by and let you take risks without doing the appropriate due diligence," said Chetan.

"Aha!" said Mr. Krishna. "Now we're finally getting somewhere!" "What do you mean?" said Chetan, his brow furrowing in confusion.

"That's the first actual piece of advice you've given me," said Mr. Krishna, leaning back into the chair. "You're absolutely right. We need to do our due diligence, always. How do you suggest we go about that?"

"Oh," said Chetan, taken aback by this sudden shift in tone. "I do have some ideas, I suppose."

"Fire away," said Mr. Krishna, crossing his arms and looking at the consultant with razor sharp focus. Chetan was startled by the man's ability to make people feel like they had his undivided attention."

"I'm assuming you've already factored in basic cost-benefit analyses," said Chetan. "But at the same time, we need to see how the costs and benefits of signing up street vendors stack up against the numbers for brick and mortar establishments."

"Right, right," said Mr. Krishna, stroking his beard. His eyes started twinkling as he said, "So you agree, then? The street vendor idea has some legs?"

Chetan gaped and then laughed. "Why, Mr. Krishna! I do believe you just pulled a fast one on me!" "Maybe so," said Mr. Krishna, smiling slyly. "Go on, then. Tell me how we can make it happen."

***

Radha, Mukesh and the rest of the team chatted happily as they approached the conference room for the end of day meeting, but Salman lagged behind. He was nervous about what he'd find in that room, with the seemingly unstoppable force that was Mr. Krishna going up against Chetan, the immovable object.

Just as he expected, he found the two of them arguing heatedly when he entered the room.

"We can't pull back that much on street vendor sign-ups," said Mr. Krishna. "The whole point is to expand aggressively and be innovative. Why try anything new at all if we're going to settle for half-measures?"

"I've given you the numbers," said Chetan, tapping on a piece of paper between them as he spoke. "I've told you how unlikely it is that you'll get anywhere close to 80% sign-ups in the city, like you're expecting. All of the cash you'll waste on a futile endeavor will be better left untouched for a rainy day."

"Should we come back later?" asked a timid Salman.

"Oh, hello Salman," said Mr. Krishna, wheeling his chair around and sighing. "No, no. Chetan and I were just finishing up our chat. Come in, everyone. Sit down. We have a lot to discuss."

The team filtered in and took their respective seats, with Chetan notably standing up so that Salman could have his chair. The consultant leaned back against the wall as Mr. Krishna spoke.

"Well, after much arguing and back and forth, Chetan and I have finally come to an agreement," he said. "While our consultant has acknowledged that the street vendor sign up plan has significant merits, I can see his point about doing too much too fast. I've made a decision. We're going to pursue street vendors, but only in these four districts."

Mr. Krishna pressed a button and the screen behind him came alive. The city's map was displayed, with four areas highlighted.

"So, that's the Central Business District," said Salman, pointing at the center of the map. "And I see you're also including the two wealthier parts of town, as well as the area around the university."

"That's right," said Mr. Krishna.

"It's a sensible approach," said Salman. "But shouldn't we maybe avoid the posh areas and focus instead on other areas with heavy foot traffic?"

"It's Chetan's belief that the wealthier residents of the city will more likely order food from an app," said Mr. Krishna.

"I see," said Salman, reserving his doubts for later.

"I've put my faith in Chetan," said Mr. Krishna. "And he's put his faith in me. This is now the next stage of our development team. I expect to see you all here first thing tomorrow morning so we can lay out a plan for execution. You're all dismissed. Have a lovely evening."

Chetan approached Mr. Krishna as the team filed out. They both shook hands firmly, with Chetan saying, "I appreciate you taking my advice into consideration. I won't let you down."

"I'm sure you won't, Chetan," said Mr. Krishna. "I look forward to working with you."

With that, the consultant left the room, leaving only Mr. Krishna and Salman behind. The business advisor looked at his boss warily and said, "Sir, I couldn't help but notice how much you had to compromise your plan."

"Oh?" asked Mr. Krishna distractedly. "Whatever you mean?"

"Something tells me that you wanted to go in for more districts," said Salman, "but Chetan convinced you to avoid the risk. And the whole strategy of targeting affluent neighbourhoods seems like his idea, too."

"We both came up with the ideas, Salman," said Mr. Krishna. "Two heads are better than one."

"Are you sure we even need him?" asked Salman. "I apologize

if I pressured you into hiring him. We're perfectly capable of doing this on our own if you prefer."

"Oh no," said Mr. Krishna. "You were completely right. It's always better to have a specialist, someone who actually knows the jungle and can read the signs."

"Is this another one of your tiger metaphors, sir?" asked Salman, with a chuckle.

"Indeed it is!" said Mr. Krishna. "My point is this: even if he's negative all the time, he can provide us with an alternate perspective. And that's immensely valuable."

"Alright, sir, whatever you think is best," said Salman, adding cheekily, "Honestly, I'm just glad the two of you didn't beat each other up."

Mr. Krishna flashed him a grin. "We started off at each other's throats, came to a bit of an accord in the middle, and then bared our claws again at the end. Guess that's business for you!"

The boss and his business advisor laughed heartily, the noise of their merriment echoing through the now empty office.

CHAPTER 7

"The Dhikala Zone," said Arjun, leaning out from the jeep. "Seems like a whole other planet, doesn't it?"

"Definitely," said Lakshmi. She looked around, gaping at the lush forest on all sides. "I'm so glad we came here. It's gorgeous. Wait... ah!"

She whacked her arm and pulled away her hand to reveal a bloody mess with a crushed mosquito at its center.

"My god, it's enormous," said Arjun, leaning in. "Don't you have mosquitoes in the city?" asked Manoj, laughing. "Of course we do," said Lakshmi. "But they're not *nearly* as big as this guy. Arjun! Your neck!"

Lakshmi smacked Arjun at the base of his neck, eliciting a sudden cry from him, followed by a ginger rubbing of the area. "Got it!" said Lakshmi with a cackle. "Thanks," said Arjun. "But did you have to hit *that* hard?"

"I wanted to make sure I got it," said Lakshmi, making a face as she wiped off the sticky remains. "Lord, how much blood has it sucked? My palm smells like iron."

"Better get used to it," said Manoj. "They're the ones that actually live here. We're just visiting."

"They can show a bit more hospitality!" said Lakshmi, scratching at the rapidly inflating welt on her arm.

"By the way I'm still not sure if the monkey calls were coming from here," said Manoj, gazing at the foliage around them, "but I guess we have no choice but to experiment."

"That's how we get to the finish line," said Arjun. "We have to keep experimenting until something sticks."

"And you have to admit, we've seen an awful lot of monkeys ever since we came here," Lakshmi quickly interjected, hoping to offset any further tension between her husband and the driver.

"I'll admit that," said Manoj. "I just wish the weather was nicer."

"Oh, I hear you, Manoj," said Arjun. "So hot and humid. I thought the air would be cooler at this time of year!"

"It usually is," said Manoj, "at least as far as I've heard. This weather now is truly bizarre." "Well, at least we have a few hours to rest," said Lakshmi.

"Four hours, to be precise," said Arjun. "Then we have to start exploring again."

"I'd love a longer break after all those days we spent exploring the other side of the forest," Manoj grumbled.

"Well, perhaps if you'd taken us to the right spots we would've spotted the tiger already," said Arjun icily.

"How is that my fault?" said Manoj, incredulous. "I'm just the driver. You're the one that's supposed to tell me where to go."

"Okay, boys, cool your jets," said Lakshmi. "We're here now, and there's a good chance we are finally headed in the right direction."

"Sure," said Arjun. Manoj silently stepped out of the jeep and began setting up the tents.

Lakshmi came up to her husband and hugged him. "I know you're annoyed," she said, "but you can't let it get to you."

"I wish I could just stay calm, Laksh," said Arjun. "I just can't help wondering how many opportunities we missed because Manoj is slow."

"You can't blame him," said Lakshmi. "He's in an unfamiliar environment." Arjun stiffened in her embrace but said nothing.

***

Three days in the Dhikala zone, zero tiger sightings. Arjun was getting antsy. He paced around the tents, hands clasped behind his back, lost deep in thought.

"The monkey calls are so unreliable," he said. "At first, it seemed like they were coming from every direction, but even when we figured out where they were, we kept running into dead ends. I just don't get it."

"How did it happen last time?" asked Lakshmi, "Maybe we can just do what you did before."

"I bloody lucked into it, didn't I?" said Arjun. "I don't even remember what I did exactly. I just remember the thrill of the hunt, the anticipation. I remember failures, too, but each one brought me closer to my goal."

"Tell me something," said Lakshmi. "Were you expecting to find the tigress when you did?" "No," said Arjun, slowing his pace. "I guess not. I was just exploring, I'd almost given up hope." "So why give up hope now?" asked Lakshmi. "We're doing everything right, I think."

"I wish we had more certainty," said Arjun. "Everything is so vague. I could've sworn that I had seen her in the area around that guest house."

"You know she's probably dead, right?" said Manoj. Arjun swiveled around to look at him. "What did you say?"

"Tigers only live about ten to fifteen years," Manoj continued. "So not only is that tigress of yours dead, but her cubs are probably gone too."

"Arjun," said Lakshmi, cautiously eyeing her husband as he straightened, looking fit to burst.

"You don't know that," said Arjun. "Not for sure. And even if she's dead, there are many, many more tigers in the jungle. We don't have to find her, I'd settle for any of them. I'd be overjoyed, actually."

Manoj shrugged. "I was going to bring this up when we were coming here, but you were so excited. I didn't want to disappoint you. It's not just that your tigress is dead, by the way. Tigers in general are exceedingly rare, and it's not likely that you'll see one."

"So why in the bloody hell did you agree to this?" said Arjun, his words ringing out like shots fired.

"For the money, I suppose," said Manoj, "and... oh... I don't know. All your talk of adventure was intoxicating. But that doesn't change the facts."

"You know what, Manoj?" said Arjun, cutting the driver off, "Why don't you head back. Leave the jeep, head back on foot. You're fired."

"Excuse me?" said the driver. "You expect me to *walk* back to the guest house?"

"Yes," said Arjun, his voice frighteningly calm. "In fact, I don't think I ever want to see your face again, so why don't you just leave the forest entirely. Go back home to your TV and your boring life. I'm done with you."

Manoj simply looked at him, crestfallen, as Lakshmi stood up and put her hand on her husband's back. She led Arjun away from the makeshift camp and said, "Arjun, you can't just send him off like that."

"Take his side again, why don't you!" Arjun exclaimed.

"Why are you even here if this is frustrating you so much?!" Lakshmi shouted back.

"Forget it," said Arjun, raising his arms. "I don't care. Do whatever you like. I'm going for a walk."

He stomped deeper into the forest, and Lakshmi watched as his figure receded and was swallowed by the trees.

***

Arjun winced as a branch scratched his arm. The foliage was denser here, and more dangerous as a result. He looked back and realized he couldn't see the camp behind him anymore. How far had he gone?

He smacked the tree branch and ducked as it swung back towards him. Standing up and gasping, he looked around. What was he doing? Why was he acting this way? He didn't know. Did he care?

The tigress is always out of reach. Dancing in his dreams, with all her cubs frolicking around her, tumbling through the grass and over each other. He knew she was dead, of course. He'd known it all along. But to hear it said out loud...

There were more tigers in the jungle, there had to be.

On he trudged, stepping gingerly over sprawling tree roots. The jungle was the true master here, and an unforgiving one at that. It demanded respect from every visitor. Arjun was no different.

He noticed the air entering his lungs. Through the nostril, down the trachea, into the inflatable balloons that somehow extracted the precise component his body needed to survive. The air was so clean here, none of the smog and smoke and fumes of the city. None of the noise either. The air was perfectly still, so much so that the faintest rustling of leaves rang crystal clear.

Oh, thought Arjun. *That's probably how we can hear the monkey calls from so far away.*

He ventured further into the forest, taking everything in. The smell of the damp earth was intoxicating, as was the sheer solitude. Just when Arjun began to surrender to the feeling of being completely alone, the silence was disturbed by voices to his left.

He turned and saw a group of four people making their way through the trees. "Hello there!" called the man in front. "Are you on your own?"

Arjun smiled wearily. "Not anymore."

"Well, it's a good thing we showed up," said the man. "Awfully dangerous to be alone out here! I'm Rohit, by the way."

"Nice to meet you, Rohit. I'm Arjun. Arjun Mishra."

"What brings you to these parts, Mr. Mishra?" Rohit asked.

"Technically speaking, I'm searching for a tiger," Arjun replied. "And please, just call me Arjun."

"Oho!" said Rohit. "What a coincidence! That's *exactly* what we came here for! First time?"

"Not quite," said Arjun, although it's been so long that it might as well be."

"Harder than you remembered?" Rohit asked.

"Considerably," said Arjun.

"Well," Rohit began, "I'm proud to say that after many days of searching and dozens of failures, we *finally* managed to spot one."

"You what?" said Arjun, nonplussed. How could this man have done what he'd failed to do?

"Trust me, it wasn't easy," said Rohit with a laugh, turning to his party of two women and one other man. They beamed back, with one of the women saying, "Rohit was about ready to give up, but then we heard something heavy slinking around behind us. Before we knew it, this absolutely *enormous* tiger was before our very eyes."

"Oh, it wasn't that large," said Rohit, chuckling. "It was no more than two years old. The little guy has a lot more growing to do, but that just goes to show how utterly massive these creatures can get."

Arjun sank to his knees. "I'm amazed," he said. "I've been here for days and I haven't gotten *any* sign of a tiger."

"Oh, I'm so sorry dear boy," said Rohit, crouching down and putting a hand on Arjun's shoulder. "I'll say again, it was one of the hardest things I've ever done, but infinitely rewarding in the end."

"How was it?" Arjun asked, dreading the answer. Rohit and the other members of his group shared a knowing, joyful look. "It was the most perfect thing we've ever seen."

Arjun didn't respond, choosing instead to ponder the soil between his knees as he slumped lower. "Are you really alone?" asked Rohit, craning his neck. "How about you come join us for a meal?" "I'd prefer to stay here," said Arjun dejectedly. "Don't have much of an appetite." "Are you sure?" Rohit asked again, giving Arjun a look of concern.

"Yes," said Arjun shortly. "Please don't let me stop you."

"Well, if you insist," said Rohit. He stood up and began to lead his group away, but turned around while he was still within earshot.

"You know, if we saw a tiger, that just means you're more likely to see one too," he called out. Arjun looked up and met his gaze, watching Rohit shrug and say, "It's always best to stay optimistic."

Rohit departed with a wave, leaving Arjun to the thoughts swirling in his head. He felt a mixture of envy, anger and disappointment. The man hadn't seemed like a particularly adventurous sort. Just another tourist from the city. Yet he'd seen what Arjun so desperately craved, and it clearly made him as happy as Arjun thought it would.

That's when it hit him.

Arjun stood up and began to sprint back towards camp. As he ran, he wondered if he'd strayed too far to make it back, but the trees eventually thinned and he spotted the blue and yellow tents in the distance. Quickening his pace, Arjun arrived at the campsite and keeled over, gasping as if he'd just climbed out of the ocean.

***

"They're bloody everywhere!" screamed Lakshmi, frantically waving away a seemingly endless procession of massive mosquitoes.

"Just put some more of that lotion on," said Manoj. Lying against the thick root of a tree and languidly picking his teeth with the nail of his pinky finger, the driver looked like the physical embodiment of calm.

"It doesn't bloody work, does it?!" said Lakshmi, wide eyed. "Even my sleeves can't keep these damned things out. They poke right through. Since when can mosquitoes bite you through your sleeves?"

"They've adapted to the jungle environment," said Manoj. "Survival of the fittest. Or in this case, the biggest."

"How are you so at ease?" asking Lakshmi, tucking her shins

beneath her thighs in a vain attempt to keep the bloodsuckers at bay. Scratching idly at her ankle, she continued, "They must be biting you too."

"They are," said Manoj, "but we have big boys like these in my hometown, too. Been bitten by them since I was a kid. Don't even notice it anymore."

"That's a useful skill to have," said Lakshmi.

"It's a skill born out of necessity and only useful so far as the necessity remains," said Manoj. "I'd much rather not have the necessity in the first place."

"Well, that's fair," said Lakshmi. "Where exactly are you-wait, what's that?"

She stood up and screwed her eyes, looking at the darkness between the trees.

"Manoj," she said. "Manoj!"

"What?" asked the driver lazily.

"I think there's someone coming," said Lakshmi. "Get up! What if it's a thief?"

"Can't do much if it is," said Manoj, placing the back of his forearm on his eyes. "Better to just give them what they want."

"Excuse me?" said Lakhsmi, her voice turning shrill with fright. "Why are you *always* so bloody *casual*? Can't you see I'm scared? Can't you just take something seriously?"

Arjun burst through the bushes, sprinting at them as if chased by a demon. He skidded to a stop a few feet away from Lakshmi and bent over, gasping as if he'd just emerged from the ocean.

"Are you alright?" Lakshmi cried, rushing to his side and rubbing his back. Manoj watched from his perch on a stray log, making no effort to stand up and join them.

"I just met someone," said Arjun in between gasps, "They saw a tiger."

"What?!" said Lakshmi. "When, where, who?"

"Just now, in the forest, doesn't matter," Arjun replied, his voice ragged and his breathing even more so. "Do you know what this means?"

"What does it mean, Arjun," Lakshmi asked, tears welling up. She'd never been so worried about her husband, in her life, and in her panic, she failed to understand what he was trying to say. Manoj, on the other hand, understood perfectly and began to laugh. Upon hearing him, Arjun began to laugh too.

"Can someone tell me what on earth is going on?!" said Lakshmi, her eyes dancing between the two laughing men.

"Why, it means I was wrong!" said Manoj. "There are tigers in the forest, after all!"

"You're goddamn right," said Arjun. "And we're going to see one. No matter what happens, we are going to find a tiger and see it in all its glory."

"I think you might be right, my friend," said Manoj, walking up to him and slapping him on the back. "By god, I think you might be right after all."

CHAPTER 8

Mr. Krishna folded his arms, a slight frown creasing his forehead as he addressed the latest hurdle. "Our 15-minute delivery service is revolutionary, but we're hitting a snag with high labor costs in the USA. It's a different ball game when compared with the Philippines," he explained."

Salman leaned in, his voice laced with concern. "The cost structure is indeed challenging in the States. It's eating into our margins, unlike in the Philippines, where the strategy is taking off without a hitch," he added.

Mr. Krishna nodded, "We knew this wouldn't be easy. The Philippines has welcomed our approach with open arms, and the labor market there is more conducive to our business model. We need to adapt and find a sustainable way to replicate that success in the USA."

The normally cheerful mood of the conference room seemed to have been deflated by a morose needle, leaving behind a thick, sombre silence in its place.

Salman sat at the table glumly cradling his chin on hands that simultaneously cupped his face. Chetan anxiously massaged his forehead with his index and middle fingers, dragging them towards his thumb in a listless pinching motion as he stared blankly at the lacquered table-top. Radha had the look of someone who'd just been told Santa Claus wasn't real.

In the doom and gloom, only Mr. Krishna showed the slightest bit of energy.

"It's all about perseverance," he said. "The signs look bad, I know, but we must persevere."

"Despite the team's enthusiasm, the street vendor strategy is also facing headwinds. It seemed the buzz hadn't reached the masses yet, and the streets were devoid of the anticipated chatter about our innovative solutions."

"I just don't understand how this could've happened," said Salman, speaking from his seat to Mr. Krishna's right. "Things were going so well. We signed up 153 street vendors and their orders alone brought in enough revenue to meet our goals last month, but everything just came crashing down after that."

Chetan sat silently to Mr. Krishna's left, with a sombre look that matched each member of the team seated in the conference room.

At last Chetan spoke up, "At first, it felt like we were hosting a grand party but forgot to send out the invitations. The office was brimming with ideas and potential, yet the silence was deafening outside." He continued in a quiet, despondent tone "We knew we had the strategy and the technology to make a difference, but convincing the world outside our walls proved to be a tougher puzzle. It was clear we needed a spark to ignite the public's interest and get the conversations started."

"I can't help but think that it's my fault," Salman said, breaking his silence. "Maybe we could've brought in more revenue if we'd been more aggressive and followed Mr. Krishna's older plan."

"I don't agree with you on that one," said Mr. Krishna, graciously placing a hand on his consultant's shoulder. "The entire market is cooling down. There have been mass layoffs in companies across the board. Thanks to your advice, we were able to preserve some of our capital to keep every employee on staff for the next quarter. To be clear, Chetan, this is the rainy day you told me to save up for, and I'm glad I listened to you."

The consultant gave Mr. Krishna a weak smile.

"Whatever the case may be," said Salman, "billables are declining. If the current trend persists, I have serious doubts about Project 100 Million Tigress."

"What are we going to do?" asked Radha. "This is a disaster."

"Calm down," said Mr. Krishna. "Look, we've all done extremely well so far. There's no reason we can't make it through to the end. I can see the trends just as clearly as you all, but we won't gain anything by panicking."

"That still doesn't answer my question, boss," said Radha running both hands through her thick, black hair. "I'm sorry, I don't mean to be difficult. I just don't know how we're going to achieve the target."

"Alright, how about this," said Mr. Krishna. "I'd like each one of you to tell me one thing you've accomplished in the past month."

The team stared blankly back at him.

"I'm serious, guys," said Mr. Krishna. "Salman, why don't we start with you?"

"Umm," said Salman, hunching his back and staring at his thumbs while he twiddled them. "I don't know, honestly. It's been a rough month. If you asked me a few weeks ago I'd have loads of achievement to list down, but I can't really think of anything right now."

"Nonsense," said Mr. Krishna, beaming at Salman as he leaned back against the wall and crossed his arms. "I can think of several things."

"Really?" Salman asked. "Like what?"

"Nope," said Mr. Krishna with a grin. "Come on, use that amazing brain of yours. Tell me one thing you accomplished this month. I know you can do it, just like I knew you'd achieve the countless things you can mention right now."

"I'm at a loss," said Salman, throwing up his hands. "I've felt like a complete failure this whole month."

"Alright," said Mr. Krishna. "I'll start. This month, I managed to avoid laying off my staff, even though *every* company our size has had to let go of more employees than I can count."

A murmur drifted through the team. They looked at each other, speaking every so quietly, and realized he was right.

"That's actually an incredible achievement, sir," said Radha. "We're all grateful that you didn't end up firing us."

Mr. Krishna laughed heartily. "Why, that's my job!" he said. "Though I'd certainly consider it an achievement, I really don't think it's something you need to be grateful to me for. Also, I'd like to mention that I couldn't have done it without our consultant, Chetan. Thanks to his advice, we saved up enough cash to cover payroll through till the end of the year."

Salman patted Chetan on the back. The consultant smiled sheepishly at everyone, clearly not recognizing how big of an accomplishment this was.

"Come on, Chetan," said Mr. Krishna. "Nothing is certain in the world of business. You can beat yourself up for some perceived misstep, or you can realize that your advice genuinely helped this business survive in a trying time."

"I suppose you're right," said Chetan. "It's not easy to be so positive sometimes, but it's important to see the good you've done."

"Exactly, dear boy," said Mr. Krishna, placing a hand on the consultant's shoulder.

"I guess I can think of something I accomplished," said Radha. "The app crashed for thirty minutes last week. You were out at a business lunch. Half an hour is a long time, but I was able to coordinate with Sebastian and get it up and running again faster than we hoped. We were expecting the app to be down all day, so that's one crisis I averted."

"Brilliant work, Radha!" said Mr. Krishna. "Thanks to your quick thinking and coordination, we managed to bring in some revenue that day. All of that will go towards successfully completing Project 100 Million Tigress. Anybody else?"

"I accomplished something!" said Mukesh, smiling and raising his hand. "It happened ten days ago," he continued after Mr. Krishna gave him an encouraging nod. "Six restaurants suddenly decided to exit the app because they felt like our cut was too high. I was able to negotiate and get them to stay with a very minor increase in revenue share, but I also got them to agree to a non-compete clause in their contract."

"Amazing," said Mr. Krishna. "Mukesh, it would've been a true disaster if you hadn't stepped in, and the non-compete clause was a stroke of genius. Now, they can't sign up with any other delivery provider! Salman, come on now. I'm sure you've thought of something by now."

Salman laughed despite himself. "Yes, alright, Mr. Krishna. The coffee machine was broken the other day. I fixed it all by myself."

"Oh, come on, Salman!" said Radha, giving her co-worker a playful shove. "You're the *business manager*. You're second only to Mr. Krishna himself. You basically run operations for the entire company! Are you saying that's the only thing you accomplished?"

"Oh I accomplished plenty," said Salman with a smirk. "Liaised with venture capital to secure another financing round if we hit half our revenue goal by next year, coordinated with the Philippines team to discuss expanding into Quezon and beyond, and much, much more. But, you see, without the coffee machine our dear Mr. Krishna would never have been in such a good mood!"

Mr. Krishna slapped his knee and let out a hearty guffaw, much as he'd done so many times before, particularly on one occasion for which he was extremely grateful - an occasion which, perhaps, no, undoubtedly, was the impetus for everything he'd accomplished so far. But he had no time to think of that now.

Wiping tears of laughter from his eyes, Mr. Krishna says, "Indeed, Salman. That's perhaps the biggest accomplishment of all. Keeping me in a good mood! Of course, your work with the VC firms and coordinating our upcoming expansion are both decent wins, too."

He gave his business manager a cheeky wink and said, "A round of applause, everyone, for Radha, Mukesh, and Salman!"

The entire team began to clap, and Mr. Krishna noticed how their faces had lit up. No longer was this a room of doom and gloom. Instead, a sense of camaraderie began to permeate the proceedings, and it wasn't long before more team members began volunteering their accomplishments.

Ishaan from marketing spoke about how he maximized their advertising footprint by focusing entirely on digital ads. "Once we launched our advertising campaign in the Phillipines, it was like planting seeds in fertile ground. Slowly but surely, green shoots of public interest began to sprout."

"Our online ads were the rain after a long drought. Conversations began to bloom everywhere, from coffee shops to online forums, about First Strategy's innovative approach."

"It wasn't long before our efforts bore fruit. The once empty inbox started filling with inquiries, and our phones rang with the sound of potential clients. The advertising push had awakened a dormant market, eager to learn more about us."

Ali from finance told everybody about his tricky balancing act while managing the budget. Suresh from the developing team chimed in and expanded on Radha's victory, saying how he modified the code without any help from Sebastian to make sure the app didn't crash again.

One by one, each and every team member added something to the list. They soon began adding multiple items, so numerous were their accomplishments. All the while, Mr. Krishna beamed at them. His team, his family. He realized then and there that he had the greatest job in the world.

CHAPTER 9

Arjun strolled through the forest, taking everything in. The vastness of it simultaneously overwhelmed him and calmed him.

It overwhelmed him because he thought he might get lost at any moment. It calmed him because no matter where he ended up, he'd still be in this sprawling, untamed jungle. He felt it was where he was meant to be.

Arjun needed the serenity of the forest. It had been ten days now, and they still hadn't gotten close to the tiger. At one point, they saw claw marks on a tree, but no jungle cat lurked in its surroundings. The marks had been left long ago, it seemed.

The other day, Arjun could've sworn he heard the sound of a monkey in fear. It wasn't a normal warning cry. Such a desperate, urgent shriek would only come if it spotted a tiger. And yet, when he, Manoj and Lakshmi sped in its direction in the jeep, they found no tiger in its path.

He was frustrated. He'd been frustrated for a while. This jungle was where he was supposed to be right now, he knew it, but he couldn't help but wonder. What was he even doing here? Was he really trying to catch a tiger, of all things? He had a wife to think about a job back home. He had everything anyone could possibly want in life, but he still felt that there was something missing.

It wasn't missing from his home life. Lakshmi was the perfect partner, and she made him feel wanted. He made her feel safe, and in doing so, he acquired a sense of accomplishment that no amount of money, fame and success could measure up to.

His work life was no different. Arjun Mishra was a titan of his field. His subordinates looked up to him, and his co-workers respected him. Perhaps there was the barest semblance of dissatisfaction, the feeling of being in a rut, but it was easy to forget when he immersed himself in the hustle and bustle of the office.

Arjun breathed in a lungful of pure forest air and exhaled it in a weary sigh. Whatever piece was missing, it belonged to a part of himself that he had yet to recognize. Could there be more to life than a loving wife and a good job? What else could he possibly need?

He walked on. The jungle, endless, lush, breathing like a giant organism, seemed to welcome him into its embrace. Or was he walking into the gaping jaw of a creature that desired his end?

The latter seemed just as likely as the former. If he failed any more than he already had, this jungle may very well end everything he knew about himself.

Step after step after step. Arjun reached up and slid his hand along a heavily leafed branch, pulling it along for a moment and then letting it snap back to its original position. *Oh, how things return to their rightful place,* he thought. *Oh, how they resist all attempts to change them. The branch will point where it's meant to point. Try to alter its direction and you'll snap it clean off.*

Arjun was beginning to realize that he'd walked deeper than ever before. There were no paths here, not even animals disturbed the forest's heavy slumber. He was in the belly of a giant, and he felt comfortable there. He had no idea how he'd get back, but he didn't care.

All of a sudden, the crushing silence was deflated by the distant sound, sharp and stuttering. Arjun turned to the direction it came from. *What on earth was THAT?*

He heard it again. Staccato and sharp, like a marching drum played with a needle against his eardrum. He felt the hair on the back of his neck stand on end.

People told stories of ghosts in the jungle. They spoke of malevolent spirits, ghosts of people who died well before their time. He suddenly began to worry about not knowing the way back.

There it was again. Arjun realized it had a familiar pattern to it. It had an organic quality, as if it came from within his own body. *No wait,* he thought, *someone else's body!*

He then realized what it was: a chuckle. Someone was *chuckling* in the middle of the forest.

More questions erupted in his mind, weeds in his already untended garden, but Arjun was possessed with the overpowering need to run towards it. He had to find out who this mysterious chuckler was, and why he was laughing in the first place.

As he ran, the direction of the chuckle changed. Suddenly it seemed to be right behind him. He turned and saw nothing but more forest. Empty, save for the trees.

The chuckle drifted in, now from his right. Then his left. Then, in an instant, it was right above him.

Arjun looked up. A man, sitting in a lotus position on the thick branch of a tree, looked down at him. "How do you do, kangaroo?"

"Kangaroo?" asked Arjun.

"Now he will say he's not a kangaroo," said the man, hopping from one branch to another. He hooked his knees around the branch, hung down, leveling his face with Arjun's, and said, "But if not a kangaroo, who are you? Tell me the truth!"

"Why, I'm Arjun," said the owner of that name. "Might I ask who you are too?"

"Yes, do!" said the man, a gleaming smile parting the dense bush of his salt and pepper beard, crow's feet forming as he said, "But tell me, what is the difference between many and few?"

"I'm... I'm not sure how to answer that," said Arjun.

"Pah!" said the man, releasing his hooked knees from the branch, somersaulting down and landing on his feet with the grace of a cat. He was wearing a faded kurta that had once been a deep orange, and his trousers were hitched around his calves. "Such a great rhyming game we had begun to play. Why spoil it, hmm?"

"I didn't realize we were playing a game," said Arjun.

"Why, it's all a game!" said the man. "Look around you. You are in a vast playground. This is where purposes are born, but also where they die." He leaned, eyes widening, and stared at Arjun intently. "Be careful which one you choose."

"I'm sorry, but you still haven't told me who you are!" said Arjun, his pulse pounding as his voice rose.

"Krishna's the name," said the man, clasping his hands behind his back. "But my friends call me Mr. Krishna."

"Mr. Krishna?" said Arjun with a laugh. "That's not usually a last name."

"Last, first, what's the difference?" said Mr. Krishna, gazing up at the trees and slowly starting to walk away. "I only believe in the here and the now, there are no winners or losers. All medals are gold!"

"Right," said Arjun, glancing around. "Well, I was curious about why you were chuckling?"

"Should I not?" asked Mr. Krishna, his brow furrowing. "What reason have I *not* to chuckle, hmm?" "What reason did you have to laugh at all?" asked Arjun.

"Funny that," said Mr. Krishna. "Why would chuckling need a reason, but not chuckling need none? Why is not chuckling the default state? I say we should be chuckling at all times, until of course we have a reason to stop."

"That's an odd way of seeing things," said Arjun, raising his fingers to his chin. "But I can see your point. Sometimes it's good to laugh."

"Exactly!" said Mr. Krishna, raising a finger. "Finally, you're getting it. Now, it's my turn to ask a question."

"What question is that?" asked Arjun. "Why are you lost?" asked Mr. Krishna, returning his gaze to Arjun.

"That obvious, huh?" said Arjun with a sheepish chortle. "I suppose I lost track of the time and wandered further than I intended."

"Haven't we all, haven't we all," said Mr. Krishna, suddenly distracted by something on the bark of a tree. He rushed towards it and let crawl onto his finger a caterpillar, with dark brown lines across its back. "Look how the creature blends in," said Mr. Krishna. "It's learned to adapt to its surroundings. Shall I ask it to teach you its wisdom?"

"Ah, I see," said Arjun, folding his arms. "You're some kind of pretend sage or guru. I'm not paying for some cookie-cutter spiritual advice stolen from a magazine."

Mr. Krishna threw his head back and laughed loudly. "Money?!" he spluttered, doubling over and clutching his stomach. "Oh please, please don't try to offer me any of that stuff. You can't even eat it!"

Arjun gave him a confused look. "Sorry, that was rude of me," he said.

"Of course, you're being rude," said Mr. Krishna. "You're lost! That must be stressful for you. Especially since you're not just lost in this forest, you're lost in life."

"Am I?" asked Arjun. "I was actually thinking about how good I have it."

"Have it good, you do," said Mr. Krishna, "but still, you feel a touch of blue."

"I'm not starting that rhyming thing again," said Arjun with a begrudging smile.

"Pah!" said Mr. Krishna again.

"What do you mean about me being blue?" asked Arjun. "That's another thing I was thinking about just now. Are you reading my mind?"

Arjun laughed as he said it, but he soon became serious when Mr. Krishna took several large steps and came face to face with him. "Being lost, being blue, these are some of those things that we'd best not chuckle over. Serious business, they can be. Especially if left untreated."

"Are you saying I should see a therapist?" asked Arjun. "That might be useful," said Mr. Krishna. "But first, you must know the way." "The way back to my camp?" asked Arjun. "The way forward!" said Mr. Krishna with another bright smile. "Oh, you were speaking metaphorically," said Arjun.

"I'd say it's quite literal," said Mr. Krishna, twirling around and drifting away again. He eventually settled on the root of a tree. Arjun sat on the ground in front of him. He didn't question why he did it. He just knew it was what he was supposed to do.

"First," said Mr. Krishna, placing his hands on his knees, "tell me why you're here." "I'm here to find a tiger," said Mr. Krishna. "Nonsense," said Mr. Krishna. "Again!" Arjun pondered. "I'm here because I saw a tiger as a boy, and I want to see it again." "Warmer," said Mr. Krishna. "Try again."

Arjun sat cross-legged for what seemed like hours, days, years, or maybe just seconds. Time lost all meaning as he thought harder than he'd ever thought in his life.

"I'm here because I want to feel like the world is new and infinite again," said Arjun.

"That, my friend," said Mr. Krishna, "is a profound thought. One well worth exploring. What's keeping you from your goal?"

"I keep looking for the tiger, but I can't seem to find it," said Arjun.

"Go on," said Mr. Krishna.

"I'm worried that I made the wrong choice by coming here," said Arjun. "I'm worried that I dragged Lakshmi into the jungle and put her through so much stress for nothing. I'm worried about so many things. I don't know what to do."

"The first and most important thing you must know is yourself," said Mr. Krishna. "After that, you must know your duty. What is your duty?"

"To care for my wife," said Arjun.

"Her being here is a sacrifice, wouldn't you agree?" asked Mr. Krishna.

"I do," said Arjun. "Maybe that's why I'm so worried... she's subjected herself to 10 days in the jungle. If we don't see the tiger after all of that..."

"So your worry isn't that you're not doing your duty at all. You're worried about not doing it right," said Mr. Krishna. "This is a good thing. It means you are on your path."

"But how do I walk the path correctly?" asked Arjun.

"You start with devotion," said Mr. Krishna. "You are here because you need to be here. Stop wasting time worrying and surrender. Be here, now. Do what you are here to do. Let Lakshmi help you. She should be with you right now."

"I don't even know why I left her behind," said Arjun, burying his face in his hands.

"You are scared that she'll witness your failure," said Mr. Krishna, "but the only true failure is to reject your duty. You have not failed yet."

"But what if I *do* fail?" asked Arjun.

"The path to failure is paved with selfishness," said Mr. Krishna. "Let go of the self. Look at those around you. What do they need?"

"Lakshmi needs me by her side," said Arjun. "And what of the other?" asked Mr. Krishna.

"Manoj?" asked Arjun. "I... I suppose he needs compassion. Respect."

"You never wondered what he needed before now," said Mr. Krishna. "You have taken a step in the right direction now. Congratulations."

"Thank you," said Arjun. "I really should be kinder to Manoj." "Do you know why you haven't been kind?" asked Mr. Krishna. "Please tell me," said Arjun.

"You are seeking a detachment that you sorely need to walk the path," said the sage, "but you're not aiming it correctly. Be detached but from yourself. Be intertwined with others. You must see your feelings and judge them before you feel them. You must disperse the clouds in your mind. Only then will you be able to move forward."

Mr. Krishna stepped down from the branch, crouched, and placed a hand on Arjun's shoulder. "And do you know what you will find if you move forward?" he asked.

"What?" asked Arjun, gazing up at him.

"Yourself," said Mr. Krishna, smiling serenely, eyes twinkling kindly. "It's a circle," said Arjun. "It ends right back where it started." "No first or last," said Mr. Krishna. "Stand still. Breathe. Feel. See." "Breathe, feel, see," said Arjun. "I understand."

Mr. Krishna lifted his hand from Arjun's shoulder and stood up, wincing as he stretched his knees. "These old bones can't stay in one position for very long," he said. "I must go. Have a lot of walking to do."

"You're going?" asked Arjun. "But you only just got here!"

"Such is the life of a traveler," said Mr. Krishna. "We have oh so many places to be! Farewell, Mr. Mishra."

"I'd have expected you to rhyme as you left," said Arjun with a laugh. He looked down, contemplating the soil beneath his legs. "Wait," he said, snapping his neck up. "Wait, how did you know my last name?"

Mr. Krishna was gone. Arjun had barely looked down for a second, but there was no sign of the man. He got up and looked around. Not a trace, as if he'd vanished into thin air.

Arjun sat back down, utterly disoriented. He then remembered the sage's advice.

Breathe

He took a deep breath, slowing drawing the crisp air into his lungs. He'd never realized how wonderful this could feel, the simple act of breathing. What other incredible experiences was he taking for granted?

Feel

He lay back down on the dirt, noting the grainy softness at his back. It was dense but surprisingly fluffy, at least on the surface. Inside, he imagined, it was considerably more tightly packed. He noticed the stillness of the ground, something he'd never have experienced in the city where everything was always vibrating. He realized that there were twigs underneath him, but he was too comfortable to remove them.

See

Arjun looked up. He'd never lain back and looked at the sky here in the forest. It was blue, clear, pristine. The trees created the perfect porthole from which to view it, framing it as if in a painting, and the green leaves made the sky even more vibrant.

A monkey leapt from one tree to another, a dot of brown streaking across the blue. Arjun laughed. Monkeys. So unreliable.

Up in the trees, seeing things from so far off. If only he could be up in the trees, he'd see the tiger from miles and miles away. *Wait a minute...* Arjun sat up so fast that he pulled a muscle in his back. He clutched at the twinging ache, gasping and screwing his eyes shut. He soon pried them back open and looked upwards again.

Miles and miles away...

"The monkeys see them from miles away!" he screamed, his voice echoing in the forest. "They're too far off! Their warning calls... oh my god... of *course*... we're not tracking the damn tiger, we're tracking the bloody *monkeys*,"

Arjun whooped with laughter, suddenly feeling no pain as he clambered to his feet. "No more monkey calls," he said. "Need to get back to Lakshmi. We can't listen to the monkey calls alone anymore. They mislead us. They mislead us! No *wonder* we haven't found the tiger yet! The monkeys are way too far! We need to listen to prey on the ground. What, though, I wonder? Oh, Lakshmi will have an answer! I know it, I know it! Or Manoj! By god, the fellow really can surprise you, I'll bet my life he'll know what to do! But I have to get back to them. I have to get back."

He set off in the rough direction he'd wandered from. He didn't need a compass. He knew exactly where he was supposed to be.

CHAPTER 10

It felt as though the team was living in that conference room. For weeks they'd been on high alert, with every team member refusing to leave for the fear that they'd miss something critical.

Only Mr. Krishna split his time between the conference room and his office, where he claimed to be working on something to help them through the crisis. Four days later, he barged into the conference room and exclaimed, "By god, I've done it!"

"Done what, sir?" said Salman, rubbing his red eyes.

"Alright people," said Mr. Krishna, turning on the screen, connecting it to his laptop and pulling up a file. "May I present to you, my pride and joy, my greatest creation, my magnum opus, Vidya Vista! Or V, for short."

"Umm, sir?" asked Radha. "What is it?"

"It's a data analysis tool," said Mr. Krishna, opening up the UI. "Look at this. I designed an algorithm that will parse all the data we're getting each day and sort it based on importance. We make decisions at random sometimes. We need to our process. Automate it."

"That's an interesting idea," said Chetan. "What are the parameters?"

"It's essentially a risk assessment tool," said Mr. Krishna. "I heard what you said about risk, Chetan. It stuck in my head. This tool will take all of our data and make projections that calculate risk and forecast revenue."

"You made this from scratch?" asked Salman. "We could've bought a tool!"

"That tool would've been made for general use," said Mr. Krishna, waving his hand. "We need something specifically catering to our goals. Besides, it would've cost money to get a commercial license for a tool like this. We're running short on that, remember?"

"I honestly don't know what to say," said Chetan. "You made this in four short days?"

Radha stood up and started clapping. Salman joined her, as did Chetan, and soon everyone was on their feet giving Mr. Krishna a round of applause.

"Now, now, team," said Mr. Krishna. "I was doing my job the same as all of you. And I think all of our jobs might be a bit easier now. Look, we can stop wasting so much time debating and just base all of our decisions on these forecasts."

"That is such a relief," said Salman, leaning back and sighing.

"We've just been reacting to the world this whole time," said Mr. Krishna. "Now we can be proactive. We can predict things! From now on, every decision will be data driven."

"We've been making data driven approaches, though," said Radha defensively.

"Ah, but we've been using the wrong data!" said Mr. Krishna. "If interest rates are low, you borrow, but if they're high, you save. Get those things mixed up and you're in for a world of hurt. And that's just what we've been doing. Our rapid expansion was based on bullish market trends, but we're in a bear market now. Capital is fleeing in every direction. We were listening to the wrong signs!"

"Of course!" said Salman, burying his face in his hands. "That makes so much sense."

"I can't believe I didn't realize it," said Chetan.

"You were in the ballpark," said Mr. Krishna. "You just didn't realize that our entire approach needed an overhaul yet. You would've gotten there eventually, Chetan! I only figured it out because I had you tempering my risk taking approach."

"You're too kind, Mr. Krishna," said Chetan. "I just wish we could solve all our challenges like this."

"Well, we can figure that out now," said Mr. Krishna. "Everybody, I need you to list down your challenges and how you're facing them. We're going to see if V can help you in any way."

"Umm, sir?" said Salman, standing up and approaching the boss before continuing in a conspiratorial whisper, "Are you sure we should be micromanaging the team like this?"

"It's not micromanaging, Sal," said Mr. Krishna. "Everyone has their own personal struggles. That's why I'm asking them to write it down instead of saying it in front of the group. I've realized, I've been a tad selfish here. I need to pay attention to what everyone else is going through. That's the only way we'll get to the finish line."

"Not long left until the end of the year," said Salman, eyeing everyone furiously scribbling things down.

"We have as much time as we need," said Mr. Krishna. "We just need to try our best. As long as we're on the path, we'll never fail."

CHAPTER 11

∽∽∽

Breathe. Feel. See.

This had become Arjun's mantra ever since that fateful meeting, and it had taught him more than he could've imagined.

Active breathing had helped him manage his anxiety, allowing him to expend the built up stress and replace it with cool, calm, fully oxygenated tranquility. Seeing was a bit trickier, because he technically saw all the time. And yet, he realized that he often didn't see as clearly as he thought.

His eyes were too often unfocused, and therefore unaware of the visual input they were receiving, and subsequently prone to misreading them. He'd started to feel a deep unease when looking at the forest. It reminded him of his failure to see a tiger. It reminded him of the seemingly impossible task that lay before him. Most of all, it overwhelmed him with its sheer size.

Now, he quite literally saw the forest for the trees. He paid attention to the shape of each leaf and their varying shades of green. He noticed the texture of the tree bark. And this made him realize that not all the marks he saw in the bark came from tiger claws. They could be from anywhere, perhaps even from other tourists, which told him that he'd been paying attention to the wrong signals.

His myopic obsession with catching the tiger made him misinterpret the signals. This was important. Now that he knew, he could filter out the noise. At least *some* of these marks must have been made by tiger claws. They bore the distinct characteristics of their razor-sharp appendages. He had to be more discerning, more careful, more focused.

Seeing is simply a mechanism for collecting information. How he interpreted that information was up to him. He had to see properly, with intent, and the path would appear before him. He could think of no better example of this than the way he now saw Lakshmi.

For several days now, the sight of Lakshmii filled him with shame. He felt guilty for bringing her to this place, where she was forced to spend hours applying lotion to fend off monstrous mosquitoes, where there were no showers to relieve the sticky residue left behind by all-encompassing humidity.

Now, he saw those things for what they were. Sacrifices. Lakshmi was here for him. She was experiencing the many discomforts of the jungle to help him meet his goal. It was up to him to make it worthwhile, by getting them to the finish line, and then by seizing the first chance to do the same for her.

He also saw Manoj more clearly than before. The poor fellow, neck deep in an adventure he'd never asked for. Arjun felt a burning need to pursue his goal relentlessly, if only so that Manoj could go back with a story for his children.

And of course, to see the look in Lakshmi's eyes when she finally saw that tiger.

Out of these three monosyllabic tips, offered to him by a man who may very well have been a hallucination, a phantom, a spirit of the forest, he felt that middle tip was the most potent. He was surprised, shocked, utterly vexed by how much he felt every second of every day.

Inside, his flow of emotions was at times, a rushing river and, at times, a trickling stream, but the flow was constant. As he felt consciously, he began separating each emotion, analyzing it, and optimizing it. If he had no choice but to feel, he would make sure to intimately know each feeling and what it truly meant.

It had been two days since his encounter with Krishna of the Forest. In those two days, Lakshmi and Manoj had heard the story of the meeting with disbelief, expressed gently by his wife and scornfully by the driver. Both forms of expression quickly shifted to concern.

"You're seeing things," said Manoj. "That's a big concern. Are you taking enough water with you?" Arjun realized that he hadn't, in fact, been taking enough water.

"I'm not saying you didn't see him," said Lakshmi, "but maybe you should take a camera next time? That way you can take a picture to remember him by!"

Lakshmi no doubt suggested this so that Arjun would see the fictional nature of his forest sage with his own eyes. Nevertheless, it reminded him that he did need a camera in case he spotted the tiger, in case he found a sign worth pursuing, or indeed, on the off chance that he met Mr. Krishna again.

"The sun can get quite hot," said Manoj. "You should take a cap, too, to protect yourself from heatstroke."

This was yet another thing that Arjun certainly needed, something he hadn't thought of yet in his obsession to find the tiger. So far, he'd only considered bringing a pair of binoculars along, but now he had an entire arsenal of tools to consider next time.

Their sudden realization about the monkey calls, on the other hand, couldn't have been more positive. Their eyes lit up as it all clicked into place.

"No wonder we haven't found the tiger yet!" said Lakshmi.

"That's exactly what I said," Arjun replied, encircling his wife's slim shoulders with his arm. "We need to think of another animal that tigers prey on. Something that roams on the ground. That will be more accurate. Any ideas?"

"I mean..." said Lakshmi, her voice trailing away. "What would cry out loud enough for us to hear?"

"Monkeys are the loudest," said Manoj, scratching at his beard. "Hard to find anything that compares."

"Okay dear, thank you," said Arjun, congenial in his mockery.

"Wait a minute," said Lakshmi, "that's it! A deer!"

"A deer?" asked Arjun. "Would that work?"

He looked at Manoj, who seemed lost in thought. "Actually," he said, "yes it could. It very well could!"

"Brilliant," said Arjun. "A deer will see the tiger up close. If we keep an ear out for it, we'll definitely find our way."

But Arjun didn't intend for Lakshmi and Manoj to accompany him. He wanted them to rest, to take the sights in, and to give him the adrenaline rush when he surprised them with a confirmed location of the tiger. Once he knew where to go, he would take them along. For now, however, he had to venture out alone.

And so he entered the forest once again, more optimistic than ever before.

***

The vast expanse of the forest stretched out before Arjun, pulling him in with such a great force that he couldn't help but walk deeper into it. He felt a chill creeping into the air, floating down from the tops of the trees. He looked up. The sky was greyer than he thought it would be. A mist was forming3. He walked on.

His ears strained for any sound that might point him in the direction of the tiger. *What was that?* he thought. There was a faint rustling coming from nearby, accompanied by the sound of giggling.

It can't be.

Arjun cautiously approached the sound, which seemed to be coming from the man he never thought he'd meet again, the man he thought might not even be real. Behind the trunk of a massive tree, he found Mr. Krishna sitting gracefully in lotus pose on a rock.

He was watching a caterpillar crawl over his finger, chuckling as it slithered its way around. Without looking up, he said, "Hello, dear Mr. Mishra. How do you do?"

Arjun snorted. "I thought I'd never see you again?" "And whatever made you think that," said Mr. Krishna.

"The way you disappeared, I suppose," said Arjun. "It felt like you just vanished into the jungle. What is it with you and caterpillars anyway?"

"Perhaps I did vanish," said Mr. Krishna, "perhaps I didn't. And the caterpillar, dear boy, is one of my favorite creatures."

Arjun crouched down in front of Mr. Krishna and wrapped his arms around his knees. "Are you going to make me ask?"

Mr. Krishna smiled widely. "Now that you have, I shall answer. I love the character because I think we can all learn a lot from it. *You* can learn a lot from it."

"Every answer of yours just raises more questions!" said Arjun. He realized that this would've exasperated him not too long ago, but now, he felt the push and pull of Mr. Krishna's fluid, rhythmic sentences and he felt it was much easier to let go.

In other words, he breathed, he felt, and he saw, and nothing else mattered. But he also felt that this was just the first of the many lessons Mr. Krishna wanted to teach him, so he relented by asking yet another question.

"And what exactly does the caterpillar have to teach?"

"Patience, dear boy, patience," said Mr. Krishna, standing up and walking to a drooping leaf. He placed the caterpillar on the verdant foliage. Arjun followed him and watched its light green, brown spotted body disappear into the leaf.

"The caterpillar lives a hard life," he said. "It's weak, nearly defenceless. It must survive until it can enter the chrysalis, and then it emerges, transformed. Its patient, determined journey ends with another metamorphosis, and that's precisely what you can achieve as well."

"By being patient?" asked Arjun, raising a thoughtful finger to his chin. "And I'd transform into the proverbial butterfly that can catch a tiger?"

"The *metaphorical* butterfly," said Mr. Krishna, "and it's not the only metaphorical thing. The same goes for the tiger. It can be a beautiful jungle cat, a healthy marriage, or a fruitful career. But you must be willing to enter the chrysalis and wait within it patiently until you are ready to emerge."

Mr. Krishna leaned in. "You know that you are in the chrysalis right now".

Arjun did, indeed, know this, though he only realized it at this moment. The forest was his chrysalis. But what was he turning into?

"You are turning into whatever it is that you need to become," said Mr. Krishna, as if he read his mind. "But you must know, the metamorphosis is just the first step."

"What comes next?" Arjun asked.

"Failure," said Mr. Krishna.

"What?" sputtered Arjun, nonplussed. "After all that?" "That's when you're ready for failure," said Mr. Krishna. "But... I've been failing this whole time," said Arjun.

"Yes, and you've failed at failing," said Mr. Krishna. "Failure is not an end. It is a beginning. It is an opportunity. Failure is solid gold, each time you achieve it, you learn something that success could never teach you. Until you become the person you're meant to be, you won't even know what to fail at, and so you will never learn the lessons that will open your eyes."

"These lessons," said Mr. Krishna, "will take you by surprise. You will strive to reach the pot of gold at the end of the rainbow, only to find out that you have a deep love of rain, and that you'd prefer to stand in it drenched and dancing and delighted, and that the gold wasn't even real in the first place."

"So I'll never find the tiger?" asked Arjun, his face falling. "I came out here hoping your advice would help me catch it."

"Oh, it will," said Mr. Krishna. "It just won't be the tiger you're expecting. Maybe it'll be a tigress, who knows?"

Arjun thought to tell him that the tiger he was looking for was actually a tigress, but realized there was no point. The tiger, tigress whatever it was, he would learn of its true meaning in time.

"Do you think there's still a chance for me to see it?" he asked.

"Oh, you will see something," said Mr. Krishna. "Something that will change your perspective. Just remember... there's more than one way to catch a tiger."

"Really?" said Arjun, his eyes lighting back up. "I sure hope so." Mr. Krishna clasped his hands behind his back and started to walk. Arjun followed at a short distance. "Your hopefulness betrays your fear," he said.

"I'm not afraid... I think," said Arjun, hastily adding that last bit when he felt the faint twinge of trepidation in his heart. "Okay, I see what you mean. I'm afraid of failure. I still don't see the benefits it can provide."

Mr. Krishna turned around and smiled beatifically. "What if I told you the secret to defeating fear?"

"Is there such a thing?" Arjun asked sceptically.

"Indeed, there is," said Mr. Krishna. "Strategy." Arjun gave the sage a puzzling look.

"Strategy is the enemy of fear," said Mr. Krishna, "for fear is born out of uncertainty. Your metamorphosis shall be the key to learning the secrets of strategy, dear boy. You came to this jungle unprepared. Now I see you with a camera, binoculars and all the tools of the trade. I see you have packed a bottle of water. You forgot even this simple but essential item in our previous meeting. I also see that you brought a cap with you."

"Yes," said Arjun. "My driver, my friend, Manoj, he said that I might get a heatstroke if I didn't bring it along."

"Sound advice," said Mr. Krishna, "but oddly irrelevant in the current climate, no?"

"Well, I had no idea that the air would get so misty," said Arjun.

"Aha!" said Mr. Krishna, his eyes widening as he raised a crooked finger. "And therein lies the problem. You prepared for one eventuality. What of the others?"

"Should I learn how to predict the weather, then?" asked Arjun, scowling.

"Conditions can change at the drop of a hat," said Mr. Krishna. "You don't want to get caught in the rain without an umbrella, now do you?"

Thunder clapped in the skies above, and sheets of rain began to fall onto the forest.

"Wha- how?" asked Arjun, covering his head with his arms in vain. "It was foggy just now."

Mr. Krishna laughed gleefully, spreading his arms wide and looking up at the sky. "At the drop of a hat, dear boy! Now drop that hat, it's of no use to you. Come hide with me under the tree, I shall reveal what you cannot see."

"Please, no more rhyming," said Arjun, rushing after Mr. Krishna and taking cover under the densely packed leaves. The air was suddenly chilly, and Arjun wrapped his sopping-wet arms around himself and shivered.

"Always be prepared," said Mr. Krishna. "Adopt this strategy and there will be nothing to fear."

"But how can I plan for every contingency?" asked Arjun through chattering teeth. "I'd never find the time!"

"Well you must make the time!" said Mr. Krishna, shouting over the roaring downpour. "Count the hours in the day. Set aside time for a specific task. When the time expires, move on to the next task. Keep yourself moving, ever forward, ever onward, but keep your direction constant. Remember that there is no first or last. You will get to your destination when you are meant to reach it. But you must work for it. You must make the time."

"I wish it was that easy," said Arjun. "But sometimes the task before me is so vast. Like right now, I want to spot a tiger. That is a mammoth undertaking. I can't just *make enough time* for it, it always runs out when I least expect it."

"You are not simply trying to spot a tiger," said Mr. Krishna. "You are coming to the forest, setting up camp, planning, making a list of tools, exploring, learning, growing. Each of these is an individual task."

"So... I should break my tasks down into smaller chunks?" asked Arjun. "Is that what you're saying?"

"What I'm saying is that you already have the answers," said Mr. Krishna. "I'm just here to remind you of what you already know!"

He started walking into the rain.

"What are you doing?" screamed Arjun. "Are you crazy? You'll catch a cold!"

Mr. Krishna only laughed. He walked forward serenely, turned to face Arjun, then started walking backwards, his arms outstretched. "Emerge from your chrysalis. Embrace every failure. Plan for every twist and turn your path will take. Make time, Arjun, make time. For your wife, for your life. You will be going home soon!"

"But I haven't even seen the tiger yet!" Arjun screamed at the top of its voice.

"It'll be waiting for you!" Mr. Krishna called back. "You just won't know you're looking for it until you find it!"

And with that, Mr. Krishna disappeared into the rain. Arjun thought he could hear a faint humming in the distance, but maybe it was just the wind through the trees. The rain was making the ground muddy, squishy, unstable. There was no way he'd be able to get back to Lakshmi and Manoj in these conditions.

Arjun sat down on the soft ground and took a deep breath. He saw that the rain had slowed somewhat into a gentler pitter-patter. He closed his eyes, and lost himself in that noise. The feeling of it washed over him, sweeping away everything he was and everything he knew. At that moment, he was just a man, in the forest, listening to the rain.

Such a simple pleasure, yet one he'd never thought to savor before.

Arjun suddenly laughed. He just realized that he'd forgotten to ask Mr. Krishna for a picture. The words he spoke, the rain, his own state of mind, all of it had distracted him too much. Even so, Arjun couldn't help but lose himself to the sound of the rain.

CHAPTER 12

The office was alive in a constant flurry of motion. Salman sat at his desk, his hair in a state of disarray, which he contributed to, with frequent sweeps of his hair through the curly strands as he furiously typed out reports.

After spending sixteen straight hours at her own desk, Radha had fallen asleep, her head laid down on a pile of papers as she loudly snored. Mukesh was sitting upside down, his feet pointed at the ceiling as he rested his legs against the wall, his back against the floor as he waited for Pulse Media, one of the agencies they worked with, to take him off hold. Chetan stood in front of a whiteboard, his sleeves folded up, his expression one of intense concentration as he intently stared at the various strategies written in front of him.

Mr. Krishna weaved his way through the commotion and reached Radha, placing his jacket on her sleeping form. She stirred slightly and pulled it closer around her before snoring again. He straightened up and said, "What say we call it for today, team?"

"Call it?!" said Salman, his voice a high-pitched shriek, "V's spitting out too much data for that. We have to constantly strategize. Just two months left until the end of year, sir, and we have another 23 million to earn to hit the target!"

"Right you are, Sal," said Mr. Krishna, "but look at poor Radha. She's exhausted, and so are you."

"We have managed to note down practically every customer complaint," said Chetan, stretching as he walked towards them, "thanks to Mukesh over there."

Mukesh gave the group a thumbs up and a sleepy smile as Pulse Media's hold tone played in his ear.

Salman stood up and rubbed his red, sore eyes. He placed his hands on his hips and looked up at the large, TV-sized touch screen that allowed them to interface with V. "I still don't like the earnings projections. At this rate we'll be ten million short by Christmas."

"A few months ago we were expecting to be 25 million short," said Mr. Krishna, "but we've managed to overcome that with two months to spare. I'm sure we'll figure it out."

"Oh my god!" Mukesh yelled all of a sudden.

"I'm up, I'm up!" screamed Radha as she jolted upright. Salman rushed over to her side to calm her down.

"What is it, Mukesh?" said Mr. Krishna.

Mukesh scrambled to his feet, saying, "I just got off the phone with Pulse. They told me Citadel Bank is taking all of its advertising in-house."

"Oh god," said Salman, fetching Radha a glass of water as she rubbed her eyes groggily. "That's bad."

"Now, now, calm down everyone," said Mr. Krishna, gesturing with his hands. "It could mean a lot of things."

"Citadel is one of their biggest accounts," said Chetan, horror dawning upon his face. "And Pulse is one of our... I mean *your* biggest accounts. If Pulse goes under..."

"Hey, I think we're getting a bit ahead of ourselves," said Mr. Krishna. "Pulse has other accounts, and so do we. Besides, advertising is just one of our revenue streams."

"I don't know, Mr. Krishna," said Chetan warily. "I kind of agree with Salman. This is bad."

Salman rushed to the touch screen and swiped at V's interface. "Look at this," said Salman, pointing to a graph. "I made V compile this three days ago. Mid-sized agencies like Pulse have lost 13% of their clients. I wasn't too worried because none of our partners lost clients, but now... what if the trend continues? What if our other partners end up losing major accounts, where would that leave us?"

"Look," said Mr. Krishna, "there's more than one way to catch a tiger. Let's say Citadel leaves Pulse. Does that mean they won't need digital ads anymore? It's not the 90s, *everyone* needs digital ads, and we're one of the hottest platforms out there right now. They want a broad digital presence, so they'll *have* to work with us, right? If anything, this gives us a chance to establish a direct relationship with them."

"That'll be tricky," said Mukesh. "I don't know if Pulse would see it as us swiping their client."

"Hmm, I don't know about that, actually," said Chetan, folding his arms and stroking his chin, his brow furrowed. "Seems like Citadel has already made the decision. We're just trying to secure our own interests. Don't see anything wrong with that!"

"It just... feels like such a massive task ahead of us," said Salman.

"It's not one task," said Mr. Krishna. "It's a lot of little ones. Call Citadel, for starters, when you have the time. Do it with Mukesh so he has some back up. There will be other small tasks, like the daily management and maintenance of the app, customer complaints and queries, and bookkeeping. Break it all down and you'll be surprised at how easy it will be for us to keep going."

"Why do I feel like there's a predator prowling behind us," said Mukesh, "and that it's getting closer by the minute."

"That might just be because you're stressed out," said Mr. Krishna. "We've had a rough few months. You're in survival mode, all of us are, and that means we start seeing predators everywhere."

He started walking back to his office and said, "Not every sound in the jungle is a predator. Sometimes it's just the wind in the trees."

Mr. Krishna entered the office, sat at his desk and watched his team through the glass wall. He'd known for several weeks now that the revenue target was becoming harder to reach by the day. This latest setback, while not insurmountable, essentially confirmed what he'd known for quite some time, but hadn't had the heart to tell anyone.

They weren't going to make it.

He felt an odd sense of peace at the acknowledgement, though he'd initially thought he'd be angry about it. He looked around his office, returned his gaze to the team outside and smiled.

"The inconsistency was clear as day; every meal was a gamble. Some days, the stew was a symphony of flavors, and on others, it was as bland as cardboard," lamented Salman.

"Our customers' furrowed brows were becoming all too common, as the unpredictable quality of our dishes left them dissatisfied," Radha observed with concern.

"It was like every cook was following their own map to treasure, but none of them led to the gold. The variance in taste, quantity, and quality was our biggest hurdle," Mr Krishna reflected during the team meeting.

As much as he'd wanted to finish Project 100 Million Tigress, he felt like what he'd gotten instead was something far, far more valuable. He watched his team bustling around, talking animatedly. He watched Salman bring Radha some food and coffee, which she had sleepily consumed while she checked her emails. He watched Chetan and Mukesh chatting animatedly, undoubtedly coming up with strategies to keep the project alive.

"Who knows?" said Mr. Krishna to himself. "Maybe we'll get there after all. But for now..."

He got up and opened the door to his office, shouting, "Okay team. I think that's enough for today. Everyone, there's plenty of food in the kitchenette, help yourselves if you like. Let's wrap things up and try again tomorrow."

The team murmured their assent and began the process of packing up for the day. Salman joined Radha with a slice of pizza on his plate and a can of Coke, bringing one for his co-worker as well. Chetan and Mukesh joined them, and everyone in the office coalesced into groups that talked amongst and with each other. The conversation flowed organically, everyone feeling comfortable enough to speak their mind.

It was a warm feeling that filled Mr. Krishna that night, at 11pm, after a long, hard day at work. He was lucky to be here, lucky to manage this team. And he wouldn't give it up for anything else in the world.

CHAPTER 13

They had been in the jungle for two weeks, and they had found no sign of a tiger. Arjun had realized a couple days ago, when he had his final conversation with Mr. Krishna, that they might not find the tiger after all. He hadn't seen the sage since then, but he somehow felt his presence wherever he looked. In some moments, he could swear he heard the sound of the guru's giggling echoing through the trees, but it never came from the same place twice.

Despite that, Mr. Krishna had proven less elusive than the tiger Arjun so desperately wanted to see before leaving. It was at this point that he decided enough was enough.

That morning, he'd told Lakshmi and Manoj that it was time to pack up and go home. Manoj had reacted with audible and visible relief, chatting happily as he packed up the tents and made sure everything was in order. Arjun had never seen the driver being so efficient, and he wondered if he'd put the poor fellow through something he'd never wanted in the first place.

Lakshmi, on the other hand, expressed her relief much more quietly. She laughed quietly at Manoj's jokes, took any opportunity to slip her hand into Arjun's, and helped with the packing. Had she been forced into this adventure too? Arjun couldn't say for sure, but he knew he had to do something to make it up to them.

"Hey, guys," he said when the packing was done. "Why don't we just head into the forest one last time?"

"Really?" said Manoj. "We should leave, I think. No point in sticking around any longer than we need to."

"I just think we should let ourselves enjoy the jungle's beauty before we leave," said Arjun. "We've been so focused on finding the tiger that we never really let ourselves have a nice time! Or rather, I didn't let us relax. Let me make it up to you."

Lakshmi once again folded her hand into his. "If that's what you want, I'm with you," she said. "Manoj, you can stay back if you like."

"No, no," Manoj grumbled. "I might as well tag along. One last time, like you said."

They began heading deeper into the forest, Lakshmi continuing to hold Arjun's hand, Manoj standing on Arjun's other side with his hands clasped behind his back. As they walked, they spoke about the many things they'd seen since they came here.

"Manoj, I learned more about bird calls from you than I ever thought I could," said Lakshmi.

"That's true," said Arjun. "You have a knack for these things. I'm surprised, I didn't think a driver would know so much about birds!"

"It's just a passion of mine," said Manoj. "Sometimes when I have nothing else to do, I like to go birdwatching."

"I thought you spent all your time watching TV?" said Lakshmi mischievously.

"Oh, I like to mix it up sometimes!" said Manoj, laughing. "Maybe that's why I agreed to come here with you two."

"I'm glad you did," said Arjun. "We couldn't have done it without you." "Done what?" Manoj asked. "We never even saw the blasted tiger!"

A monkey call rang out above. The three of them started laughing. "Do you want to go running after it?" Lakshmi said to Arjun with a nudge.

"Not a chance," said Arjun, placing a protective arm around his wife.

"Thank goodness," Manoj sputtered. "For a second I thought you'd have us running on another wild tiger chase."

Another sound rang out through the trees. The trio looked at each other. "Was that..." said Lakshmi.

"It sounded like..." said Arjun.

"A deer!" said Manoj. "Come, follow me!"

He started running to the east at a speed neither Arjun nor Lakshmi had ever seen him reach before. They followed him at full gallop, leaping over branches and rocks with the ease of an Olympic athlete. A sense of purpose had given them unprecedented control over their limbs, their hearts beating against their chests aggressively.

"There it is again!" cried out Manoj as another deer call rang out. "We're getting closer!"

They picked up pace and spotted an opening in the tree line up ahead. As they approached it, the dense vegetation gave way to a massive clearing where they keeled over and gasped.

Arjun looked around frantically. "Can you see it? Can anybody see it?"

His head swerved from side to side, but there were no signs of the orange and black-streaked jungle cat he was after. "It's not here!" he said, scanning the body of water in front of them. "It's not here!"

"Arjun," Lakshmi said, tugging at his sleeve. "Arjun, look!"

Arjun's gaze ventured to where she was pointing, and he gasped.

Elephants, both big and small, were standing in the water, sucking the water through their trunks and ejecting it above so that it landed back as rain. The baby elephants were splashing around in the water. Arjun saw one little guy being pulled by a larger elephant, who he assumed was its mother. The baby looked unwilling to enter the water. His mother gave him a push, he landed in the shallow end and stood up, flapping his ears as his friends rushed towards him.

There were gharials as well, basking in the sun a fair distance from the elephants. Birds flapped around them, some landing on their heads and flying back up at the slightest movement. The reptiles lazily soaked up the sun's warmth, seemingly too content to attack the birds that were in clear view.

There was no violence here. No predation. It's like they had stumbled into a place where the animals had called a truce, vowing to maintain peace so that they might enjoy the forest they all shared. And it was as though Arjun, Lakshmi and Manoj had been drawn to this sanctuary, where the water was clear and the sun's rays not too hot and the air was cool enough that their sweat evaporated quickly.

"Well, would you look at that," said Manoj. "It's beautiful..." said Lakshmi.

"It really is," said Arjun. "It really is."

They approached the animals in the clearing and sat down in front of the pond. The animals didn't seem to mind their presence. They were too busy living their lives. The trio sat for what felt like hours, silently admiring the scene.

"I've never seen anything like this in my life," said Manoj. "I can't wait to tell my kids!" Arjun laughed and patted his back. "Guess you got some good stories to tell after all." "Yeah," said

Manoj. "I have to admit, this is something special. Wait, take a picture of me!"

He stood at the pond's edge as Arjun took out the camera and pointed it at him. After some guidance, Manoj stood in such a way that he seemed to be pointing right at the elephant that was on the other side of the pond. Arjun snapped the photo and showed it to Manoj.

"My god, I look rough," said the driver. "I wish I'd shaved! But send this to me, won't you? I want to show my kids."

"I will," said Arjun. "I'll send you all the pictures we took here."

"Thank you!" said Manoj, turning back to face the water. He gazed at the animals admiringly, taking it all in.

Lakshmi rubbed her hand against the salt and pepper stubble that now covered half of Arjun's face. "You're looking a bit scruffy too, mister."

"Do you like it?" asked Arjun, rubbing his face as well. "I might keep it." "I like it a lot," said Lakshmi. "Time for a change, you think?"

"Yeah," said Arjun. "I also think... and you can tell me if I sound crazy... but I think I want people to call me Mr. Krishna."

Lakshmi laughed. "So you want to be Arjun Krishna?"

"No, no," said Arjun. "Just Mr. Krishna. I'm still Arjun Mishra, but also Mr. Krishna. I know I'll never see him again, but maybe this way I'll keep him alive in my heart."

"He had a huge impact on you, didn't he?" said Lakshmi. "I wish I could've met him. You know, he actually sounds a bit like you."

"Maybe he was me," said Arjun. "Maybe he's the butterfly." "The what?" asked Lakshmi, laughing.

"Never mind," said Arjun, smiling. "Manoj!"

The driver turned around.

"Ready to leave?" asked Arjun.

"Leave?" said Manoj. "Now? But we just got here?" Lakshmi and Arjun laughed heartily. "Remember when all he wanted was to leave?" asked Arjun. "Yeah," said Lakshmi. "You changed his perspective. You have the ability to do that, I've noticed" "Oh, so you notice me, do you?" said Arjun, winking at his wife. Lakshmi covered her mouth and chuckled. "Ten years of marriage and you still flirt with me."

"And I always will," said Arjun.

They sat there for some time, Manoj running around and shouting gleefully, Lakshmi and Arjun mostly sitting and watching him but occasionally joining him for a jog. They didn't get too close to the animals, but drank them in with their eyes.

Eventually, the sun had reached its peak, and they knew they had to leave. They returned to the camp, hoisted their packed belongings onto the jeep. Half an hour later, they were driving to the edge of the forest.

As Manoj drove, Arjun heard the many noises of the forest crashing into him. Monkey and deer calls, the rustling of leaves. Was the tiger still out there? Were any of these beautiful creatures still around? He didn't know, but he realized now that in pursuing them, he'd become a new man. The tiger itself was irrelevant. It was the journey that mattered in the end.

Sometime later, they exited the forest and got back onto the long stretch of road leading to it. It was surreal to be surrounded by so much open space again. The feeling was almost overwhelming, making Arjun feel a tad agoraphobic despite himself.

"I can't believe we have to get back to work," said Lakshmi. "It seems so odd after being in the forest for so long."

"The workplace is just another jungle," said Arjun.

"And what sort of tiger are you planning to catch there?" she said cheekily.

"Hmm..." said Arjun. "You know what? You have a point. What is the tiger of the workplace? What is it that I should strive for?"

"I was kidding, Arjun," said Lakshmi, giving him a look of disbelief. "You're so literal!"

"Of course I am," said Arjun. "And there literally is a tiger waiting for me at the office. I just have to figure out what it is. Project Tigress, I'll call it. Wait..."

He became lost in thought for a moment.

"Ah... I learned a hundred million things in the jungle but I just... I don't know where they fit in at work," he said.

Arjun cleared his throat and made a brief, yet significant announcement, he began, his voice steady and imbued with a newfound confidence, "you have known me as Arjun, but today marks a new chapter in my life. Inspired by the profound lessons of patience, wisdom, and courage I've learned from the jungle's majestic creatures, I've decided to embrace a name that reflects my personal transformation. Henceforth, I shall be known as 'Krishna.'"

Arjun cast a sideways glace at Lakshmi to see her reaction.

Lakshmi was surprised, though she had a feeling that Arjun was undergoing a profound spiritual transformation in the last few days but change of name was the last thought on her mind.

Manoj chimed in. "Preparedness, strategy, interpersonal conflict resolution, these are just some of the things I learned. They should be valuable, even in the fancy offices you city slickers like to work in."

"Wow," said Arjun, "that's actually so true. Work's been going well, but now that I think about it, there are things that we can try to achieve. You know what, we should shoot for the stars. We'll double our revenue next year!"

"That's insane," said Lakshmi. "That'll bring it to... what? 138 million? Even 100 million will be an achievement."

"You earn *that much?*" said Manoj, astonished.

"The company does," said Arjun with a laugh. "Not me personally. We have salaries to pay, expenses. Like you have to spend to maintain your jeep, I have to spend and maintain my company. And Lakshmi, you're right. Double is too much... but 100 million? That sounds good. A 100 million lessons from the jungle, 100 million in revenue. It fits."

"Even that's a 45% increase," said Lakshmi. "Are you sure about this?"

"Oh yes," said Arjun. "I think we can do it. And even if we don't... who knows what we'll achieve along the way?"

He rested his head against the seat. "Project 100 Million Tigress," he said. "I like the sound of that."

CHAPTER 14

While everyone was adjusting to their seats around the table, Chetan took off like he was possessed

"After a renewed effort at advertising, the 15-minute delivery promise managed to set us apart. Customers couldn't stop talking about how we're revolutionizing the convenience of food delivery." He continued without stopping. "Who knew that our quick delivery service would become the talk of the town? It's like we've hit a sweet spot for foodies everywhere," scrolling through the trending hashtags on social media.

"Seeing our branded vehicles zipping through the streets, making deliveries in record time, gives me such a thrill. It's a visible sign of our growth," Salman observed from the office window.

The sound of merriment flowed in the office as Mr. Krishna thought back to the day he changed his name. The day he exited the forest and decided to go on this wild, crazy journey, seemingly insatiable in his thirst for adventure.

He exited into the main floor and was greeted by cheers and applause. To the left, the wall had been cleared out and a banner saying "PROJECT 98.7 MILLION TIGRESS" in red paint, a tongue in cheek reference to their final revenue total for the year.

Mukesh staggered towards him, saying, "Congratulations, Mr. Mishra. Oh, sorry! Krishna, Mr. Krishna. Sorry, I forgot about your name change for a second. I think I had one too many."

Mr. Krishna placed an affectionate hand on the shoulder of his tipsy, slightly slurring team member as he walked on. "No worries at all, Mukesh. It feels pretty new to me as well, even though it's been over a year!"

He walked into the center of the floor, and his team gathered around him. Radha was wearing glasses several times too big for her face, one of the many props that Salman had procured to give the New Year's Eve Party a bit of a humorous tone. He himself was wearing a fake beard, and Chetan had allowed himself the luxury of a lush, blonde wig.

"Speech, speech, speech!" cried Salman. Soon, the entire office had joined him, quietening down when Mr. Krishna began to talk.

"It's been a great year, everyone," said Mr. Krishna. "We went from 69.3 million last year to 98.7 this year. An increase of 42%! A round of applause, please, for yourselves."

The team clapped and hooted.

"Now, I know what you all are thinking," said Mr. Krishna. "We didn't hit a hundred million. But my god, 42% in a single year, I still can't believe it. We shot for the moon and ended up in the stars. I'd say that's the greatest victory we could ever hope for. And we all gained so much else along the way, things that can't be expressed in numbers."

"Radha," he continued, looking at his lead product manager, who took off her massive glasses and looked at him with wide eyes. "Your energy and passion have inspired me throughout this journey. Without you, I doubt we would've made half as much progress as we did."

Radha's eyes welled as she smiled, the office applauding for her, and Salman giving her a friendly hug around her shoulders. She leaned her head against him as they listened.

"Mukesh," Mr. Krishna continued, "the way you handled so many clients and delegated to your team was seriously impressive. I knew I could steer the ship as long as I had you. You manage your end with vigor and enthusiasm, and that's something that I, personally, want to match moving forward."

The team applauded wildly again, hooting as Mukesh bashfully accepted the praise.

"And of course, Salman," said Mr. Krishna, beaming at his business manager. "You, my boy. *You.* None of this would've worked without you, the glue that holds us together. You, the man that I know to be my successor, if I'm lucky to hold on to you that long."

The office laughed and clapped at that, as Salman looked at Mr. Krishna almost in disbelief, his mouth slightly agape. His boss approached him.

"You taught me how to be a better manager, a better leader, because you *are* a leader, Sal. And I can't wait to see what you teach me next."

Salman rubbed a tearful eye. Radha pressed her head against his shoulder with an "Aww!" as Mukesh patted him on the back.

One each and every team member received a glowing review from their leader. When he'd gone through them all, he looked at Chetan who was hanging slightly back and watching them leaned against a desk, a serene smile on his face.

"And you, Chetan," said Mr. Krishna. "You know what? Come here, you old salt. I have to talk to you about something, and you'd better say yes! As for the rest of you... what're you waiting for? It's a party? Go on!"

The team cheered, the music was turned on, and Chetan laughed as he approached Mr. Krishna. "Gosh, a private talk, must be serious," said Chetan with a wide smile.

"Oh it is," said Mr. Krishna. "The most serious thing I can think of right now. Chetan, come work for me."

"Well I have been working for you," said Chetan with a puzzled look.

"Full time, I mean," said Mr. Krishna. "Become my COO, at least for a few years. Until Salman is ready."

"I... I don't know what to say," said Chetan.

"Say yes," said Mr. Krishna. "That's an order!"

"Well, how can I argue with that?" said Chetan, his surprised laugh making Mr. Krishna laugh in kind.

They talked for a while, the team danced, and eventually, Mukesh tipsily insisted that Chetan join them. Mr. Krishna headed back to his office and watched them, pride swelling in his heart.

One could say he felt like a bit of a tiger at that moment.

The phone rang. He picked it up to hear his wife on the other line. Lakshmi's voice flowed over him like a warm bath in the frigid winter air. Soothing, soft, silky. His favorite sound in the world.

"Why, hello Mr. Krishna," she said teasingly.

"Hello, Mrs. Krishna," he said.

"Please, leave me out of it," said Lakshmi, playfully mortified at the thought. "I'm perfectly happy being Mrs. Mishra."

"We should go to the jungle again," he said. "Yeah?" said Lakshmi. "I'd love that, actually. I want to see those elephants again."

"Should we hire Manoj?" he said, his sly smile coming through in his voice, prompting shrieking laughter from Lakshmi.

"Can you imagine?" she said. "He'd hate us for even asking."

"Oh, I saw the pictures he sent," he said. "The ones with his kids? They've grown up a lot since he first showed them to us."

"Right?" said Lakshmi. "He looks good too. Although I'm not too sure about that moustache!"

They both laughed at this, and when their chuckles slowly faded, he said, "I want to go every year, I think. If you'd rather stay at home, I'd understand. You never have to come."

"Are you kidding me?" said Lakshmi, "I wouldn't miss it for the world!

"I love you," he said.

"I love you too," said Lakshmi. "How'd it go today, by the way?"

"It was perfect," he said.

"Well, does that mean you can come home soon? I'm sure everyone needs Mr. Krishna at the office, but I miss my Arjun."

Arjun Mishra gazed out his window, took in the gleaming lights of the city below, and smiled. "Yes dear," he said. "I think, for now, I'm done."